MOTHER NATURE

Other Titles by Margaret Bacon

Fiction

KITTY
THE EPISODE
GOING DOWN
THE PACKAGE
THE UNENTITLED
HOME TRUTHS
THE SERPENT'S TOOTH
SNOW IN WINTER
THE KINGDOM OF THE ROSE
OTHER WOMEN
FRIENDS AND RELATIONS
THE EWE LAMB *
MOTHER NATURE *

Non-Fiction

JOURNEY TO GUYANA

For Children

A PACKETFUL OF TROUBLE

* available from Severn House

MOTHER NATURE

Margaret Bacon

This first world edition published in Great Britain 2000 by
SEVERN HOUSE PUBLISHERS LTD of
9–15 High Street, Sutton, Surrey SM1 1DF.
This first world edition published in the USA 2001 by
SEVERN HOUSE PUBLISHERS INC of
595 Madison Avenue, New York, N.Y. 10022.

British Library Cataloguing in Publication Data

Bacon, Margaret
    Mother nature
    I.   Title
    823.9'14 [F]

    ISBN 0-7278-5636-7

All situations in this publication are fictitious and
any resemblance to living persons is purely coincidental.

Typeset by Hewer Text Ltd.,
Edinburgh, Scotland.
Printed and bound in Great Britain by
MPG Books Ltd., Bodmin, Cornwall.

One

"Don't move," Liz said, coming out of the kitchen door to where they were sitting on the patio having breakfast. "You look such a contented old couple, relaxing like Darby and Joan, whoever they were."

"Thanks for the old couple bit," her father said, looking up at her as she stood by his chair. "And actually I wasn't thinking of moving."

"Of course not, but Mum was," she told him, leaning down to kiss the top of his head. "When Mum sees a daughter approaching, she thinks, 'I must get up and get her coffee.' Isn't that right, Mum?" she asked, going over and kissing her on the cheek. "Actually, I'm a big girl now and can get it myself." And she ran back into the kitchen.

Flora watched her go, the smile of surprised welcome still lingering on her face. Sometimes she heard other parents grumbling that their offspring treated home like a hotel once they left school, dropping in unannounced when they wanted feeding or laundering. But she felt they were more like migrating birds whose occasional visits brightened the uneventful stream of their parents' lives.

She pushed back her reclining chair and gazed around her. It was one of those unaccountable moments, she thought, when all seems well with the world, when the air is balmy and the garden fresh after its long winter sleep, when the last of the narcissi still show bright and yellow and the Japanese quince still retains its ruby, waxlike little flowers but the plum trees are already white with blossom and the apple bushes begin-

1

ning to show pink buds, fragile against the showier chalices of the magnolia. It is the time of hope when wistaria begins to send forth downy, brown spikelets that will soon begin to open slowly into the softest powdery blue and the rockery is mounded with all shades of aubretia, with sweet alyssum and creeping thyme.

Of course, she thought, you know that the weather is unseasonably mild and that late frosts might come and kill the tender fruit just forming behind the plum blossom and blacken the magnolia chalices and stunt the wistaria, shrivelling those delicate drooping buds, but you don't believe it. And even if it's true and comes to pass, nothing can take away the harmony of this moment.

"A penny for them?" Liz asked, trailing her hand through her mother's hair as she returned with her mug of coffee and sat down at the breakfast table.

"I was just thinking how lucky we are to be able to sit in such a garden on such a morning," she said, leaning forward to push the toast rack towards her daughter.

"Gosh, I'm starving," Liz said, reaching for butter and marmalade.

It's all that youthful, hunger-inducing sex, her mother thought but did not say.

"And to what do we owe the honour of this early morning visit?" Duncan asked. "And on a Saturday too?"

"Jasper had to fly to Switzerland early this morning for a meeting. Some crisis or other. So we were up betimes."

"There's a lot of Aids in Switzerland," Duncan said.

"Thank you for pointing that out, Daddy dear. Actually we practice safe sex."

"It was nothing personal. I'm just telling you. It has the highest rate in Europe. Surprising really in such a clean and orderly country."

"Of course, nobody would expect there to be any venereal diseases in a country where the trains run on time," Liz told him, laughing.

2

Flora tried not to join in, but couldn't help it.

"Look at Mum's mouth quivering. Go on, Mum, laugh. Be a devil."

Duncan looked from one to the other, gave them one of his oh-you-two looks, shaking his head, and went back to reading his paper. Liz munched away at toast and marmalade and Flora watched them both through half-closed eyes, then returned to her peaceful contemplation of the garden. Another lovely thing about this time of the year, she thought, is that there is now a little lull before the next crop of weeds push their way up, before the rockery plants need cutting back and the bulbs dead-heading. A time to savour and enjoy.

"Make the most of this," her daughter said, as if reading her thoughts. "Gran will be back from respite next week."

"We'll manage."

"Jane's mum said that when *she* was young, Gran was quite famous. Jane had never heard of her any more than I had," she went on, spreading marmalade, "I mean for as long as I can remember she's just been my dotty old Gran."

"You don't remember her before that at all?"

"When she first came to live with us I suppose I just thought that all grans were like that, you know, cheating at patience and doing crosswords. And I liked her funny hats, I remember. But I never thought she'd been famous. I mean I know she was a journalist and all that, but then there were heaps of them, weren't there? What was she famous for?"

Flora hesitated.

"Go on, Mum. Spill the beans. Was Gran a notorious courtesan or something?"

"No, and I'm not prevaricating, just trying to think what she *was* famous for. Just for being herself, I suppose. She had strong opinions about everything and a gift for expressing them. She wrote well, that's how it began, with fashion journalism."

"I suppose that's where you got the writing bit from, though there can't be much in common between fashion journalism and writing history books for kids. Anyway, go on."

"Then she got invited on to radio and television to air her views."

"Gosh, I wish you'd recorded it."

"We didn't in those days."

"Which days?"

"Well, I suppose her heyday was in the sixties and seventies."

"So she had quite a long innings?"

"By the time you were old enough to understand, she was doing much less. She was coming up sixty and though she was still very good looking, there was younger talent around. So gradually it dropped off and then, of course, she began to get confused."

Loyalty forbade her to describe the disastrous television show on which her mother lost her temper and so abruptly ended her career. It was all over a figure of speech. "There is no question of his guilt," she'd said of a man found guilty of rape. "So you feel it was right that he got ten years?" the interviewer had asked, surprised. "Of course not, he was innocent," she'd snapped back. "But, Anita, you've just said that he was unquestionably guilty." "I did not. I said that there was no question of his being guilty."

If only they'd let it go, it would have been over and forgotten, but no, they went on at each other, her mother outraged that anyone dared impugn her use of the English language, the young interviewer unable to resist the temptation of baiting her. It ended with her walking out of the studio and producers deciding that she was past coping with unexpected situations. Unflattering photographs in the next morning's papers didn't help. It was the last appearance she ever made; overnight Anita Montrose had become bad news.

None of this did Flora say to her daughter.

"But yes," she said instead. "I'm sure Jane's mother would

4

remember about her. I suppose she was one of those house-hold names of the time, like Germaine Greer."

"Oh, I've heard of *her*. She invented the clitoris in about 1969. I forget the exact date. But it didn't work out, so she went back to being a virgin."

"You're awful," Flora told her, shaking her head in mock reproof. "But I suppose it must all seem as remote to you as the nineteen thirties do to my generation. By the way, there's a croissant or two left in the oven."

"Talking of generations," Liz said thoughtfully as she returned with the croissants and settled down again at the table, "isn't it odd that you and Gran did the reverse of everyone else? I mean mostly it's the grans who didn't have careers and the mums who did, but in your case Gran had this great career and you didn't do anything much except just be a mum."

For a moment she felt stricken. *Just* be a mum indeed. That was not how the younger Liz had viewed it as she came in from school expecting – and finding – her mother always there, ready to help and encourage, to listen to her reading when she was little and later on to hear her Latin verbs and her French vocabulary. Ah well, maybe it had given her the confidence to be so judgemental now. And besides, one didn't have children in order to earn gratitude.

"Of course, there were always the kids' history books," her daughter conceded kindly, "but they weren't exactly best-sellers, were they?"

"No, but they were what I could do at home."

"Well, I shall be like Gran except that I shall keep my marbles."

She stretched and yawned.

"I'll have some great career, maybe in television, maybe something to do with travel. Jasper thinks I'd be good at publicity. But right now I'd just like to flop. Is the hammock up?"

"Yes, Duncan put it up this morning between the beech tree and the Bramley."

"The what?"

"It's a variety of apple. Cooking."

"Well, as long as it can take my weight I'm not fussy about its variety," Liz told her. "Leave the dishes. I'll do them later."

"All right, darling," Flora said, knowing that she wouldn't.

She watched as her daughter collected up some cushions and made her way down the garden, round the corner by the rose bed and into the orchard. The grass was growing fast now. Duncan had said he'd cut it this morning, but he was lying back in his chair, newspaper-bedecked and sound asleep. He'd been working very late recently and needed the rest, she thought as she began clearing the table. The lawns could wait until tomorrow. Lawns and paths and patio-making were his department; growing things was hers. He didn't like messing about with fiddly little plants, he said. And so they divided the garden between them in much the same way as they shared the rest of their life together, she reflected as she carefully removed a ladybird which was attempting suicide in the milk jug.

Two

In the kitchen, methodically stacking plates and saucers, separating them from the knives and spoons, Flora thought about what Liz had said about mothers and careers. She hadn't seen much of her own mother when she was a child. A succession of nannies had bathed and fed her, taken her to the park and then to nursery school. After that she had been put into a navy blue uniform and sent away to board.

At school they'd thought she was illegitimate, whispering behind their hands, "Flora Sutton's mother's a journalist called Anita Montrose, so she must be illegit, poor Flora." She hadn't understood at the time, had assumed they pitied her because she was plain and mousy, like her father, whom her colourful mother had left after two years' of marriage, shortly before she herself was born.

It was only after her friend Sally, drawing her away to a quiet spot behind the bicycle sheds and peering at her through thick-lensed glasses, had asked, in a whisper, "What's it like, being a bastard?" that she had realised. She couldn't bring herself to explain that her mother had kept her maiden name because of her career. Nobody else's mother had done such a thing. They didn't in those days. So it was simpler just to say that it was quite nice being a bastard really and after all Leonardo da Vinci was one too, wasn't he?

By this time her mother had branched out from writing about fashion; articles by her appeared now in magazines and the popular press on everything from reforming the welfare state to the laying out of a cottage garden. So long as there was an element of human interest, Anita Montrose could be guaranteed to find it. Editors could rely on her to produce something witty and provocative on practically anything at short notice; her views were sought on homosexuality, Sunday shopping, hunt saboteurs, breast feeding, immigration, the royal family, high-rise flats, crash diets, euthanasia and even, to her daughter's surprise, the bringing up of children.

Holidays were always a problem.

"When I was at school it always seemed to be term-time," her mother laughingly complained to her friends, "but now that I'm a parent it always seems to be holiday-time. Really, there seem to be more and more of these wretched holidays."

She arranged for Flora to go to various holiday camps, organised by philanthropic youth groups or commercial agencies. "Such fun," she'd say. "And you'll probably meet a quite different class of child. So good for broadening your outlook."

Sometimes parents of girls in her form at school were quite happy to invite Anita Montrose's daughter to stay in the holidays. "Make yourself at home with us, Flora," a mother would welcome her when she arrived. "We're very free and easy here."

But somehow she never did feel at home. It just seemed odd, this business of going down in the morning to sit around a family breakfast table, with everyone arguing about what they'd do all day, to have mothers who always seemed to be there, mostly in the kitchen, to be with girls who thought it was quite normal to have family picnics and outings, or just to have a garden to go out and play in. All of it seemed unnatural to one whose parents lived on their own in separate, gardenless flats. She tried hard to fit in, but it was a relief to go back to school. At least at school she didn't have to keep thanking people for doing her the favour of having her there.

Her father used to come to visit her at school and sometimes she spent whole days with him in the holidays, though she never stayed the night because her mother said it wasn't suitable. They would walk around the streets of London

8

together, her father and she, in a companionable sort of way, not saying much. Or they would stay in his flat and she would read while he worked on the manuscripts he brought home with him. He was a literary agent, specialising in making manuscripts more marketable. "It's amazing what he can do with a manuscript," her mother once said of him. "No other agent can touch him for turning a silk purse into a sow's ear."

A gentle man, still in love with her mother, he had an air of quiet sadness about him which she found strangely comforting. He was undemanding and she knew that he enjoyed being with her, a feeling she never had with her mother, with whom she was awkward, tongue-tied and desperately unable to please.

"I know I don't see much of you, my darling," her mother would say, "but I do give you *quality* time, not like some poor children who just have a rushed glimpse of their mothers at breakfast and tea. Now we have this lovely two hours together and you can talk to me about anything in the world. The floor is yours: tell me any problems you would like to discuss."

She could never think of anything to say. Her mother wouldn't understand; how could she when she didn't know all the everyday things of her daughter's life or the people in it? If she did screw up her courage to tell her about a problem, her mother's solution was so instant and dismissive that she was ashamed of having mentioned it. How could her mother know what it was like to be bullied?

Sometimes her mother would try to enliven the proceedings with argument. "Don't be afraid to contradict me," she would say. "After all, I may be quite wrong – I'm only human. Now this is what we'll do. I shall make a statement and you must feel absolutely free to contradict me and then we'll have a really heated discussion. Won't that be fun?"

With sinking heart, she would watch as her mother, leaning forward, her eyes bright with expectation of argument, came out with some pronouncement. She knew she would never be able to contradict it because her mother always sounded so convincing, so she would just shrug, pull a face and agree. Her mother's bright eyes would turn dull and her face and body, deprived of confrontation, would seem to sag. And Flora would know that she had disappointed her yet again.

It was always a relief when her mother looked at her watch and said something like, "Goodness, I must dash. Sorry, my darling, when we're getting on so well, but I'm due at the BBC in under an hour."

She often broadcast now; quick and articulate, she voiced her opinions wittily and succinctly on quiz shows and discussion programmes. By the time Flora got to university, her mother was famous enough for her daughter to be aware that at parties total strangers, who wouldn't have bothered with her otherwise, talked to her when they found out who her mother was.

"That's nonsense," David, her friend Sally's older brother, said when she told him. "People like you for yourself."

He was just being kind, of course. It was out of kindness that he had got in touch with her when she first came up to college and took her out in an older-brotherly, platonic kind of way. Apart from the fact that they were both kind-hearted, he didn't resemble his sister at all. He was good-looking for a start, though not glamorously handsome. He was clever too. Sally was a love but nobody could have described her as either pretty or clever. But they both had this gift of making you feel better about yourself. Just as some people have the gift of undermining.

"Look," he said now. "People wouldn't go on wanting to see you if it was just your mother they were interested in. They'd ask you out once and that would be it. The reason why they ask you again is because you're fun to be with."

Perhaps he wasn't just being kind. Perhaps there was something in what he said, because the odd thing, she observed now that she was older, was that she was a different person away from her mother. Sometimes she wished that her mother could be invisibly present when she was with other people, laughing with them and making them laugh. Then her mother might have been quite proud of her, or at least not so ashamed.

At the end of her first year, she went to France to do a vacation job in a restaurant. When she got back, her father met her at the airport and all the way in the car and over dinner, she regaled him with stories about the family she'd stayed with: how Madame, who was short, fat and very excitable, did all the work, how Monsieur was hardly ever there because he had four mistresses dotted along the coast, whom he had set up in shops at fifty kilometre intervals. His mistresses nagged and bullied him so much that when he came home he looked so hen-pecked that his family felt sorry for him and let him lie on a chaise longue in the hall drinking Pernod.

After he'd recovered and set off again for another tour along the coast, his wife would sit with Flora, shaking her head, recounting his misdeeds and telling the number of his mistresses on her stubby pink fingers. "*Une, deux, trois, quatre,*" she would say, pushing back each little chipolata-like digit in turn. "*Ce n'est pas l'amour − c'est une maladie.*"

On her last evening in the restaurant three young men had come in, one of whom claimed to speak good English. His friends listened, impressed, as he talked to her in an English so mangled she couldn't understand a word, though she pretended to, not wanting to shame him in front of his mates. "Eengleesh, Mees," he said at one point, "paper plis." Puzzled by this request she had sought out Madame who was simultaneously frying potatoes, stirring a sauce and rolling out pastry. Asked for paper, she shrugged, waved her hands in the air, shrieked for a bit, rummaged in a drawer and brought forth a sheet of writing paper. When Flora laid it in front of the young man, he looked mortified while his monoglot friends fell off their chairs with laughter, gasping, "*Du poivre, du poivre,*" as they spluttered and choked. They were still laughing when she returned with the pepper, but their linguistical friend had left in disgust.

All these things and much more she told her father until he laughed and almost lost his habitual sadness. She stayed the night for once and went to bed feeling happier and more confident than she had been for years.

"I've arranged a little dinner party for you," her mother told her on the telephone next day. "Just a small welcome-home affair. I want to show off my daughter to my friends."

There were eight of these friends and it seemed to Flora, as they sat around her mother's highly polished, silver-and-napery bedecked dining table, that the women all had a harpy-like quality. It was something to do with the way they cocked their heads to one side, a certain sharpness in their faces, alertness in their eyes, as if they were ready to peck and tussle. The men were more relaxed but, it seemed to her, watchful. She felt immediately isolated among them.

"Now, darling, tell us all about France," her mother said.

The hugeness of the question silenced her. The words rang in her ears: *all about France.* How could she tell them all about France? She looked around at them as, faces questioning and eager, cutlery suspended, they awaited her reply. It would have to be a tremendous reply, of course, to match the size of the question. She could think of nothing to say.

"Oh well," she managed to blurt out at last, when the silence was getting beyond bearing. "It was all right."

It was as if someone else had spoken; she heard the awfulness of it with their ears.

"Perhaps you'll tell us more later," her mother said, shrugging and casting an apologetic glance around the table.

"Tell us, Flora," one of the men said. "What are young people thinking nowadays? We're all so dreadfully old, you know. How does the modern student view the world?"

Another of those huge, unanswerable questions designed to silence and embarrass. This time she could only smile and shrug.

"*I* never was a student," her mother put in. "I was far too stupid to go to university."

They all demurred, of course. They looked from the soi-disant stupid mother to the supposedly clever daughter and drew their own conclusions.

Flora sat in silence as they chattered, trying to look interested in the conversation, but only just keeping tears at bay. *I'm not like this with anyone else*, she wanted to protest.

At last the meal was over and they made their way to the drawing room for coffee. At least here she had something to do, handing round cups and chocolates. Her mother delegated the serving of brandy to one of the men.

"I expect all your friends envy you," one of the women said kindly to Flora, "having Anita for a mother. It must be so entertaining for you just being with her."

"I'm not with her all that much," she replied, aware of sounding ungracious.

After that they gave up any attempt to include her in the conversation which turned to gossip about people she'd never heard of and books she'd never read. When she said she thought she'd go up to bed, nobody demurred or tried to detain her.

It was that dinner party which had changed her relationship with David.

"It was ghastly," she'd told him as they drank coffee in her room on the first day of term. "I just disgraced myself. I was stupid and dumb and boring and I let her down in front of all her friends."

"Why didn't you tell them all the things you've been telling me?" he asked, helping himself to another chocolate biscuit. "I've hardly got a word in edgeways."

"It's not as simple as that. You don't know what she's like—" and suddenly, inexplicably, she'd burst into tears.

He put down the biscuit, came over to her chair, somehow contrived to gather her up and hold her close. For a long time

13

she couldn't stop crying, the sobs welling up of their own accord, as if all the unshared pain, all the loneliness and humiliations of her childhood had built up an ocean of unwept tears which, now that the floodgates had suddenly opened, poured out uncontrollably, making her splutter and choke as she lay against him, almost drowning in her grief. At last the storm subsided, shuddered to a halt.

"Sorry," she said, moving away from him. "I can't think what came over me."

"Don't move," he said. "It's nice."

It was nice too, she realised, still snuffling as he kissed her. Surprising, but nice, to lie here in his arms in this big armchair.

"You're such a lovely honey colour," he said, his hands gently moulding the contours of her face, as he wiped away her tears, "from all those weeks in the sun. And your hair is bleached quite blond."

"The sun always does that to it," she told him, managing a smile.

"You should wear it up like this," he said, running his fingers through her long hair and lifting it up.

"No, it shows more of my face."

"But it's a lovely face," he protested. "A heart-shaped Madonna-like face, with that serious look and those huge grey eyes."

She shook her head.

"That's not what I see in my glass," she told him.

"No, of course it isn't. You just squinny anxiously in the mirror, probably worrying about how you don't look like your mother or something silly. But other people see you like this, like you really are, the one who laughs and forgets herself because she's thinking about other people and – oh, I don't know, come here."

He held her close again and she relaxed, no longer limp and tearful but warm and responsive. She had been kissed before, of course, but lightly, affectionately, not at all like this. As she lay there, his hand rested, quite casually, it seemed to her, accidentally even, on her left breast. At first she felt embarrassed for him, sure that he was unaware, and thought of trying to shift tactfully away, but gradually she realised, as she pressed gently back against his hand, that it was quite the best place for it to be and the only problem was that her right breast was now feeling strangely neglected. She moved slightly so that it might be comforted by the pressure of his other arm.

She was surprised when he immediately began to undo her dress; it was not what she had intended and she did think perhaps she should say so, but he was kissing her too hard for that. Besides, at the touch of his hand on her bare flesh, a curious shock ran through her. Or rather didn't run through her, but stayed, filling her body with quite unexpected sensations. This was a strange new world, she'd thought, full of unsought, undeserved delights, all so utterly unlike the whole of her previous existence. She lay back, eyes closed, giving herself up to pleasure, but at the same time feeling a new power, of being for the first time in her life the one who could grant favours.

When she opened her eyes, he was gazing down at her and she saw the question in his face. She said nothing, just gazed back. He must have read acquiescence in her eyes because slowly and carefully he lifted her up and carried her over to the bed. And all the time that he was undoing buttons, moving straps, struggling with hooks, while never neglecting her lips, her breasts, her thighs, she was aware that, mixed in with all the joy and sensual pleasure and anticipation of even better things to come, there was this sense of power, the confidence which comes from being wanted. And that was something she had never felt in her life before.

And so they became lovers and remained so for the rest of their time at college.

Overnight, it seemed, the problem of where she should go in the vacations was solved. She and David backpacked together round Europe, they climbed mountains in Scotland, they camped in Cornwall. Twice at Christmas they joined parties of students and went skiing. Sometimes she stayed with his parents who lived in Warwickshire where his father had a business making garden machinery. As well as Sally, there was another younger sister and brother and they all seemed to accept her as one of themselves. For the first time she felt at home in an ordinary family, as she joined in discussions around the table at meal times, or helped his mother round the house or weeded flower beds while David mowed the lawns for them. At weekends if it was hot they carried meals out into the garden, picnicking on rugs under a great weeping ash tree, and afterwards played croquet or boules with the younger children, David's parents sometimes joining in, more often sitting together under the tree reading the newspaper. And it all seemed to her idyllic; this is how I shall make a home if I ever marry and have children, she'd decided.

She'd begun to plan how her life would be; if she married, she would have a job until she had children, so that she would have something to go back to later on, but so long as they were little, or longer than that if need be, they would come first. I shall not, she vowed, put myself and my career first, as my mother did, I shall put my husband and children first, I shall make a real home for them where they can bring their friends and my husband shall be loved and supported as my poor father never was.

Her friends had laughed at her when she expressed these views. *You're so old-fashioned,* they told her, *nobody thinks like that now. It's how our mothers did things, for goodness' sake.* It had not been how *her* mother had done things, she'd thought but not said. Let them mock, nothing would shake her determination: she would either not marry or, if she did, she would make her home and family the centre of her life.

And that, she realised now, was exactly what she'd done – though not with David.

The washing up finished, Flora moved about the kitchen, putting cutlery in drawers, crockery in the big dresser at the far end of the kitchen. There was a different view of the garden from here; she stood for a moment by the window looking down towards the orchard, where she could just see the end of the hammock tied to the Bramley. Liz's legs were hanging over the side. Very relaxed, her daughter looked, no doubt weary after last night with Jasper. How much more confident and worldly-wise she was than she herself had been at that age, she thought, how much more experienced. And how different college life was now from what it had been twenty-five years ago, though at the time they had all thought themselves wonderfully liberated compared with the previous generation of women students.

Though recognised as a pair, she and David hadn't lived together at college; it was a few years before that was to become commonplace. They each had their own room but used to work together, sometimes at her place, sometimes at his. Mostly it was to her room that he came, always clutching armfuls of books and papers, sometimes flowers and chocolates as well.

"It's so much more economical than heating two rooms," he would explain, but of course they invariably ended up in the big armchair and then in bed, books neglected on the table, essays unwritten.

"After today," she had announced a month before Finals, as she sat at the table which served as a desk in her room, "I think we ought to keep apart and do nothing, absolutely nothing, but revise."

"But it's so much nicer working together—" he began, coming and standing behind her chair.

"You know jolly well that we *don't* work, that's the point. And there'll be heaps of time to be together after Finals."

"What, with you going off to Grenoble for a year?" he had asked, resting his hands on her shoulders.

"You're going to come over and see me."

"If the old man'll give me a day off."

He still hadn't decided what he wanted to do but his father

17

had said he could work in the family firm for a year, while he made up his mind; clearly his father hoped that he would make the arrangement permanent.

"I do wish you weren't going away, Flora," he persisted, his fingers beginning a gentle massage of her neck, as he stood behind her.

"I have to go, David. It's a good course and the term's practice teaching in a French school is invaluable."

"It's not even as if you were going to teach French," he objected. "Historians don't *need* to be linguists. And anyway you're fluent enough already."

"It's as well to have a subsidiary subject, everyone says so," she told him, aware that she sounded less convincing than she would have done if he hadn't been rubbing her neck like that and playing with her hair like that and fiddling with her ears like that. And generally taking an unfair advantage.

Besides, the thought of being away from him for a whole year did sometimes induce panic. She'd tried not to think about it, just remind herself that when she got back they'd go on as they were now, as if they'd never been apart. Not that she wanted to marry until she'd done her extra year's training and got a teaching job.

"Teaching?" her mother had repeated, when she told her what career she had chosen. "Well, I'm sure that's very *worthy*. But you know what they say, darling, don't you? 'Those who *can*, do. Those who *can't* teach,'" and she pulled a little face, a little *moue* of apology.

Later, on a programme in which children and careers were being discussed, she heard her mother say, "In my experience one's children can be relied upon to live down to one's expectations."

She minded less than she would once have done, now that she had David. Her mother could still wound, but had lost the power to devastate.

"We'll have to make plans about where we'll live when you get back," David had said, slipping his hands into the wide cap

18

sleeves of her dress, reaching round her back until his fingers met, gently stroking all the time.

"I shall have to be near college."

"And I shall find something near you," he whispered in her ear, as his hands moved firmly, persistently forward. "And if we're going to have this great embargo on sex until after Finals, why don't we make the most of this last day?"

From the chair to the bed wasn't very far; he carried her easily.

"When you get back, we'll be together for ever and ever," he said, undoing buttons. "Oh, I do think this is such a sensible dress with all the buttons down the front. Why don't all your clothes work like that? You will be careful in France, won't you? Don't wear anything that comes off easily, will you?"

At first she couldn't reply for laughing, later because he was kissing her. Then he was swearing at her bra, as he always did, and she was laughing again, at him and his exasperation and the warm delight of it all.

He had just won his battle with the hooks when somebody knocked at the door.

"Don't go," he ordered urgently. "Just don't move."

"Sorry, Flora," a voice called. "But it's the telephone for you. I think it's your mother."

"I'm booking a table at the Savoy," her mother told her, as she stood by the telephone in the corridor, clutching her dishevelled clothes about her, "for next Thursday. Just for the two of us."

"Oh, no, I really can't possibly. Finals start in under four weeks."

"Oh, exams, what a bore! But then a break is probably just what you need. You'll get stale if you do nothing but work."

"It's not like that—"

"A little treat is what's required," her mother interrupted. "Thursday. One o'clock—"

"I really don't want to be away from college at all—"

"It's just lunch, you'll be there and back in the day. It's not as if I was suggesting a week's holiday. I'll send a car to the station if you tell me what train you'll catch. Sorry, must dash."

David was exasperated.

"You should simply have said you weren't coming. That's what anyone else would have told their mum."

"I know, I know. With Finals round the corner I need a trip to London like a hole in the head. Oh, well, at least she isn't asking all her journalist friends. Just me."

He thought for a moment, then said slowly, "Would it be any help if I came with you?"

"Oh, David, *would* you?"

"My exams start later than yours, so I don't mind. But she may not want me. It's a bit of a cheek to invite myself when she's never even met me."

"No, that'll be fine. She's often asked to meet my friends, but I've always been careful not to let her. She probably thinks I haven't any. I'll ring and tell her."

"Later," he said, "we have unfinished business."

As she rejoined him on the bed, she'd thought once again how much easier it had been to cope with her mother since she'd confided, two long years ago, in David. Gratefully she slipped back into his arms.

Her mother was looking stunning. At the sight of her, David's eyes widened as men's eyes do when they see a beautiful woman. Or perhaps, Flora thought, observing the look, it was just with surprise that any mother of hers could be so attractive.

She was at her most sweetly devastating throughout the meal, entertaining them with anecdotes about her work, while apologising for talking shop, teasing just a little, seeing that everything they had to eat and drink was perfect.

"Now, David," she said, as she handed him his coffee, "you must tell me all about yourself. What do you intend to do when you've got this splendid degree?"

"*If* I get it," he said, laughing.

"*Ça va sans dire*," she replied, handing him the cream.

"Well, actually," he said, looking directly into her eyes. "I want to go in for journalism."

"Splendid! Join the club."

Flora was astonished. It was the first time she'd ever heard him even mention a career in journalism.

"Oh, I don't know about joining the club. I said it's what I'd like to do, but I've no connections."

"Connections!" she laughed. "Don't worry about connections. I'm saddled with connections. I'm weighed down with connections."

Then, as if pulling herself together, she went on, "No, seriously, David. I'll be delighted to help you in any way I can. We'll have a long talk about it when these wretched exams of yours are over."

It must have been a long and fruitful talk because when Flora came back to England a year later, David was assistant editor of *Men and Women*. And he was living with her mother in a love nest in St John's Wood.

Three

D uncan had woken up by the time she went back into the garden.

"Where's Liz?" he asked, putting aside the technical magazine he had been reading.

"In the hammock. She went into it while you were asleep."

"I hope she knows what she's doing," he said, "with that fellow Jasper."

"Don't worry. She's got her head screwed on the right way."

"It's not the screwing of her head that's worrying me."

"We have to accept," she told him, perching for a moment on the edge of her chaise longue so that she could talk to him more easily, "that times have changed."

"For the worse."

"Maybe. It's different now anyway. It's strange really," she went on thoughtfully, "how we make our children conform when they're little to the world as we've made it. Then they grow up and change everything and we have to learn to fit in with their world, conform to their new rules."

"I don't see why I should conform to things I don't approve of," he told her indignantly. "I can tell you that if I'd messed about with a girl of eighteen when I was Jasper's age, my father would have belted me. I've told Liz so."

"Yes, I've heard you. Often."

"Not that she takes any notice."

"But the odd thing is, Duncan," she pointed out, "that I'm the one she argues with, not you."

He laughed and said, "That's because she thinks I'm a harmless old duffer and there's no point in arguing with me."

"It's no good worrying," she told him again. "As you used to tell me when I got in such a state about Nick when he was doing that terrifying rock climbing."

"But that's different," he objected. "Nick's always been able to take care of himself."

"I remember when he first pulled himself up in the playpen, you said, 'Good. Now you can stand on your own two feet.'"

"Did I?"

"Yes, you did. And when Liz did the same thing a few days later, you said, 'Careful, darling, you might fall over.'"

He smiled, remembering.

"I suppose fathers are always like that," she said. "More protective of their daughters."

"Was your father?"

She shook her head.

"No, poor man. He was the one in need of protection. I meant fathers in normal families."

"Is there such a thing as a normal family?"

It wasn't a rhetorical question. A practical man, not cursed with imagination, he was interested in *things*, how they were made and how they worked. When it was a matter of people and how they were made and worked, he turned to Flora for illumination.

"No," she said now. "There are too many different norms."

Satisfied with this reply, he picked up his magazine and was soon back in the world of calculable things.

Flora lay back in her chair, watching him, deep in his *Electrical Review*, fascinated by the way these technical magazines absorbed him as much as a good novel absorbed her.

The attraction of opposites, she knew that was what people had said when she had fallen in love with the electrical engineer from Sheffield University, who had come to talk to the Sixth Form about careers in engineering. It was a bonus that he had been impervious to her mother. He didn't dislike

her; it was just that being a practical, down-to-earth North-
erner, he couldn't see the point of Anita Montrose, her friends
or her life style. So he was neither impressed nor alarmed by
her.

Nor were his parents, whom Anita asked out to dinner to
celebrate the engagement. She could still remember how her
mother had led the way, tall and elegant as always, looking
neither to right nor left, aware of being the centre of attention,
while Duncan's parents ambled along behind, looking round
appreciatively at the chandeliers and gilded chairs, showing
their interest in their fellow men and women by nodding to
other diners as they passed. When, during the meal, a waiter
appeared with a wooden peppermill the size of a small minaret
which he proceeded to offer to each of them in turn, Duncan's
mother had watched in amazement. "You'd think," she'd said
sotto voce to her husband, "that a grand place like this would
be able to afford more than just the one pepperpot." He had
agreed, "Where we come from," he had explained to his
hostess, "even in quite ordinary cafés you get a condiment
set for each table."

"A penny for them," Duncan said, looking up from his
reading to interrupt her reverie.

"I was thinking about the time in Les Papillons and the
episode of the peppermill."

He smiled too; they had often laughed together at the
memory of it. It was a comfortable old joke between them.

Very comfortable had been their life together, she thought
as he turned back to his magazine. It had been a marriage
without rows and never particularly passionate after the first
few years. And even in the first few years she had never felt
with him as she had done with David. But it had been a very
practical partnership, with Duncan showing his affection for
her in the things that he did for her, not in things that he said,
which was a far better basis for a lifetime of marriage, she
consoled herself in moments of doubt, than passion.

He'd changed, of course, over the years; probably more

than she had. He'd had to adjust, as he was promoted, to being less on site, more in offices, more concerned with management and finance, but that happened in every profession. He was involved in more official entertaining, more making of business contacts, which involved late nights and sometimes being away at weekends. She didn't press to go with him or to help to entertain his business contacts. She was the home-maker, the centre to which he could return and be himself. Besides, business entertaining wasn't her scene. It had never been his either and she admired the way he had adapted to it.

Of course she shared his anxiety about Liz. She didn't like the idea of her eighteen-year-old daughter having an affair with a man who was nearly twice her age any more than he did. But argument would only make her more adamant, delay the disillusion which would come in time. Liz was strong willed and would make her mistakes in her own way; the only course for a wise parent to take was to be ready to pick up the pieces when it all went wrong, as it inevitably would. Flora was sure of this; the thought gave her no satisfaction, only sadness at the pain which lay ahead for her daughter.

There was something in what Duncan had said, she thought as she lay back in her chair beside him. Liz always argued with her mother, not her father. Not that argument gets you anywhere. Once she had tried to lift her father's gloom by telling him that his wife was not worth his heartache. "Render unto Reason the things that are reasonable," his sad voice replied. "But love is not among them." He spoke not cynically, but matter-of-factly, in the manner of one quoting an unalterable, if inconvenient, truth.

She had never argued with her mother, as Liz did with her. Why not, she wondered now. Why did she never counterattack? But then her mother didn't exactly use argument, just emotional force. The only time she'd tried to argue with her they had ended up having their one and only row; it hadn't been so much an argument as an emotional explosion.

It had started out of nothing. Her mother had come to see

the new twins. After handing over expensive presents for her little granddaughter and grandson, she had looked disapprovingly around the untidy room and at her dishevelled daughter and said suddenly, "And when do you intend to go back to work?"

"But I *am* working," she'd replied, indignantly, remembering that she'd been up three times in the night, risen at six, bathed and fed two babies by ten o'clock, done the washing and hung it out by eleven, cooked the lunch for herself and her mother by one, fed the babies by two thirty and would soon be taking them to the park, after which they would be fed, bathed and put to bed when they would take it in turns to wake her up a few times before six o'clock the next morning.

"If a nanny did what I do it would be called a job," she persisted. "And it wouldn't include night duty either. So I think, yes, I do have a job already."

"I went back to work three months after I had you."

"There is no way I could afford to pay for good help on anything I could earn," Flora told her. "Besides, I want to be with my own children."

"A brain unused can become rusty," Anita warned. "I find it absurd to see talented young women, trained to have careers, spending their time wiping bottoms and mopping up baby vomit. I certainly would never have made that mistake."

"Perhaps your mistake was to have a baby in the first place," she heard herself say with unexpected ferocity. "If looking after it was so dreadful. I don't know why you had me," she added, suddenly realising that she was at last expressing a thought which she'd had many times before.

"Every woman has a right to have a child."

"Then every child has a right to have a mother. You didn't care about that, did you? Babies were boring, little children bothersome, so send them away, out of sight, as soon as possible. Boarding school, holiday clubs, other parents. Just a matter of dates and diaries. Let someone else do the looking after, anyone but you, Mother, anyone but you."

Her mother was staring at her, speechless.

A whole lot of other things, evidently stored up over the years, came pouring out.

"And you had to take David from me, you used your power and influence when I had neither—"

"I didn't take David from you," her mother protested. "It isn't as if you were more than just good friends."

"Is that what you chose to believe, Mother, or what he told you?"

"I wish you wouldn't keep saying 'mother' in that tone of voice."

"Very well, I'll tell you. You did take him from me, my best friend and my first love. You did it deliberately."

Her mother had got up suddenly and begun to pace the room.

"All right then. I did want him, but he wanted me even more. He was wasted on you. You were young and were surrounded with young men. Whereas I needed him. For God's sake I was in my forties and he was twenty-three. Of course I had other men friends, mostly middle-aged and getting tired. What women wouldn't have helped herself to him if she got the chance? Don't fool yourself that it's the natural way of things for men to be well matched with younger women. That's just about money and power. Sexually the men are humbled and the girls unsatisfied. How different the other way round. The young man exultant at the conquest. And the woman, oh, how satisfied."

She had turned and faced her daughter.

"You know nothing of the world," she said.

"Nothing of *your* world, you mean."

"Of course I knew it couldn't last," her mother went on, ignoring the interruption. "I knew he'd want a family eventually. It was bound to come to an end one way or another. But it wasn't one-sided. I made his career. And he used to

27

come back to me after he was married, when he had nothing to gain by it. All right, it hurt me when he left. I admit it. I knew it would and I was prepared to pay the price. Do you know the saying, 'God said, "Take whatever you want. Take it. And pay for it." '? Well, I took. And I paid."

"No. You took and your daughter paid."

Then slowly, as if she had just realised it, she said, "You were a rotten mother and I shall do all I can to be the opposite of what you were. That's one thing I should be grateful for, Mother; you've given me guidelines by which to judge what I should never do. Negative criteria. I hope to God that I resemble you as a mother in no way whatsoever. I'll try to give my daughter confidence, I'll let her know that she is loved and cherished for herself, not for her cleverness or her looks. She shall have respect, she shall never be belittled or made to seem stupid. In other words, Mother, I'll love her. Do you hear? Can you understand? *Love her.*"

Her mother had listened aghast to this tirade. It is the first time, Flora remembered thinking, that I've ever touched her, the first time she has reacted to anything I've said or done.

She looked older, as she sat there, staring at her daughter, her face revealing how it would look when she was really old; the incipient wrinkles were waiting to be deepened, the tired skin under the eyes would soon fold, the chin, already less taut, would slacken, the cheeks begin to hollow, to cave in as the planes of the face narrowed.

For a moment she felt sorry for her, but she pulled herself together knowing that compassion was a weakness her mother would never have indulged in. No, she would not apologise, would not withdraw a single word. And, of course, a word, once spoken, cannot be withdrawn anyway.

So she lay alongside Duncan as he read, remembering in tranquillity that great welling up of fury, how she had said all the things that had lain unsaid for years and how afterwards her relationship with her mother was subtly changed, the balance of power redressed. So that when her mother's career declined, gradually and then spectacularly, she was able to accept her and then, as the years took their even more cruel toll, their rôles were reversed and she had to be mother to this childish old woman.

She closed her eyes, enjoying the gentle morning sunshine, her earlier contentment still lingering. It's a peach of a day, she thought, the sort of day when you can forgive anyone, even your own mother.

She'd done that long ago, of course. Not that she regretted the bitter fury with which she'd attacked her that day; she'd meant every word. And she'd done what she'd said she'd do. She'd tried to be to her children everything that her own mother had not been to her. She'd supported them, always been there when they needed her, put them first in all her decisions, put her home and family before her own career, not gone back to teaching until they were both out of primary school. Not that she'd stayed long when she found how the world of school had so dramatically changed in the few years she'd been away from it. Parent power, that great myth of the eighties, had replaced parent responsibility, making adults belligerent and children unruly, while staff struggled with constantly changing curricula and wasted time on endless assessments. "You don't fatten the pig by weighing it," she told a visiting inspector before handing in her notice. She smiled now as she remembered his shocked face.

She hadn't smiled at the time; they needed the money, and the hours had suited her well. But fate had been kind and produced Mr Monroe, publisher of history books for primary schools, who needed editorial help with his new series on life in the Victorian age, work which she could do mainly at home. She'd done other similar little jobs but, obdurately putting the family first, never had a career.

She never would now, she thought with just a touch of regret. Edgar Monroe had written recently offering a proper job, writing for a series of biographies of nineteenth-century

Prime Ministers which she would have loved to do, but it would have meant spending days in London and working away from home in libraries and although the children would soon be away, she now had her mother to look after and anyway did she really want not to be around for Duncan when he might be at home, now that his work took him away so much?

A light wind was stirring; it lifted a sheet of newspaper off the ground and deposited it by her chair. She had been blown the crossword page, she noticed, picking it up. Not that she would attempt it; that had always been her mother's speciality. Cheating at patience and doing crosswords, that was how Liz had described her grandmother. Presumably it was because she was so quick with words that Anita had been good at crosswords. For as long as Flora could remember, her mother had done *The Times* crossword every day, grumbling at the hours she wasted on them, while at the same time being unable to leave one unfinished. In the sixties she'd started going to the annual competition in London and once even reached the finals. The last time she'd gone was five years ago, the day Flora realised that her mother was becoming something more than merely eccentric.

She had insisted that Flora should accompany her and enter the competition as well, despite her protests that she was hopeless at crosswords.

"Don't worry about it," her mother told her dismissively. "I'll do the enabling one and once you're in, you must just do what you can."

So, unwillingly, she'd agreed, partly, she realised with hindsight, because she was already beginning to worry about her mother going to such a function on her own.

Anita had dressed for the occasion; her long silver grey skirt was topped by a scarlet shirt and turquoise jacket. On her head she wore a matching toque hat with emerald feathers. She stalked ahead of Flora into the hotel and joined the throng of competitors.

Flora observed that they all seemed to be either very young or very old, not many were middling, as she was. One extraordinary little man looked not much more than twelve, but had a boomingly deep voice and was wearing a wedding ring. Several old ladies wore long skirts though not many were as brightly dressed as her mother, apart from one wearing a hat so bedecked with cherries and other bits of artificial fruits and blossom that it looked as if a dried flower arrangement had fallen on her head. They all seemed to know each other, kissing and shaking hands with the familiarity of people enjoying an annual reunion. Her mother greeted everyone impartially, not distinguishing between those she knew and those she did not.

They sat in rows, divided with partitions so that they couldn't cheat. Outlines of puzzles and some rough paper lay in front of each place just like school exams. Four puzzles were to be done with a break for tea at half time. Suspended overhead was a large clock marked with thirty minutes, the maximum time allowed.

A bearded young man in a green velvet jacket sat on the other side of her mother. He had a thin, pale face with fierce little deep-set brown eyes.

"Good afternoon," he said. "I think I've seen you here before."

"Indeed yes," her mother said graciously, bowing towards him.

"How's your time? I'm a twenty-minute man myself."

"That's nothing to be proud of," her mother shrilled. "Very tough on your wife."

Blessedly a bell rang, ordering them to start.

"Oh, I suppose he meant crosswords," her mother remarked to nobody in particular as she turned the paper over.

It used to be the children who embarrassed me, and now it's my own mother, Flora thought, cringing, as she too turned the paper over.

The clues bewildered her. "Contract that's set up between

banks (7)" – whatever did it mean? It doesn't matter, she told herself, I'm only here as her watch dog. I shall just sit and do nothing and hand in a blank paper at the end. But there was something about the atmosphere of the place, the look of intense concentration on the faces all around her, that brought back memories of school exams and a powerful urge to get something down. She had managed two answers when an old man a few yards away put up his hand to show that he'd finished. The clock showed that twelve minutes had passed. Twelve minutes and *he'd finished*? She hadn't even read all the clues yet.

Her mother was writing busily away. The man in the green jacket finished in exactly twenty minutes. She herself, at the end of half an hour, had managed to get five of the answers and wasn't even sure that one of them was right.

The second puzzle was easier, or maybe she was just getting the hang of things. With five minutes to go she'd solved almost half the clues. Most of the other candidates – if that was the right word – had finished already. Still, she wouldn't be completely humiliated, she thought, involved despite herself, as she pored over another clue. "Trade in the wind restricts the head (10)," it read. It began with M and had G for the seventh letter. Market something, she reckoned and the G might make it end in gust or gale. That was it: martingale. It was something to do with horses' heads, wasn't it? She wrote it in, just as the bell rang, ridiculously pleased with this small triumph.

"Tea," her mother exclaimed, jumping up and taking her hand. "Come along."

She led the way to where in the distance teacups were being laid out on long trestle tables, covered in white linen.

"Quite disgraceful," she called back over her shoulder, "that one about the wind. Farthingale indeed! Whoever would have thought *The Times* would use a word like *fart* in a crossword?"

"But it wasn't—"

"And where are the biscuits?" her mother was demanding of

a waitress who was pouring out her tea. "No biscuits, you say? No biscuits? But there have always been biscuits. For years and years, tea and two biscuits. What is *The Times* coming to? Words like fart and no biscuits."

Before Flora could collect her own tea, her mother had set off down the room. She could see the emerald feathers weaving their way between the rows of queueing heads, hear the high-pitched voice indignantly pronouncing, "Standards are slipping everywhere. Words like fart and no biscuits."

She caught up with her at last. "It couldn't have been farthingale," she told her, gripping her firmly by the arm and propelling her back towards what she now thought of as the examination hall, for the second part of the competition. "It was martingale. Farthingale has too many letters anyway."

"Nonsense, child. I've been doing this thing for years and what does one extra letter matter? There's plenty of room in those squares."

So the day always stood out in Flora's memory, the day of the last crossword competition her mother would ever enter, she who had been so quick, so clear-headed, after which came the slow deterioration, the steady downward curve, interrupted by upsurges of recovery, moments of brilliance even, which marked the graph of her mother's declining mind.

And she'd realised that she couldn't let her go on living alone, that families have to be responsible for difficult grandmothers as well as for difficult children, daughters for mothers as much as mothers for daughters, that the present is intolerable unless the past is truly forgiven. A home would have to be made for her under their roof. So Duncan had begun drawing up plans to make her a self-contained flat with a communicating door and her mother had agreed to the arrangement as if she was doing them a favour.

But, it occurred to Flora now, as she lay in her chair and looked down her garden, to wonder what it meant to say that she forgave her mother. If they were to meet in some afterlife, which mother would it be: the elegant Anita Montrose or the old woman who didn't notice that she had spilled food down her front or the vague one in between who cheated at patience and squeezed extra letters into the squares of crosswords?

The telephone rang.

"Don't move," Duncan said, opening one eye. "I'll go."

She got up, knowing that he wouldn't.

"Nick! Give me your number and I'll ring back."

"No need. Save your pennies. I'm just ringing to say I'll be back on Thursday, so I can go up to Grandma's birthday tea with you all. Got to go now. We've got this lift to London and it's waiting. Bye, Mum."

"Goodbye, darling," she said and wandered back outside.

"Your son's coming home on Thursday," she said softly to Duncan, who was dozing over his magazine.

He grunted.

Eager to share the good news with somebody, she went down the garden to tell her daughter. Liz was asleep in the hammock.

Restless now, she went back into the kitchen and began to plan next week's meals. Nick's favourite was roast lamb and apple crumble. So that was Thursday night's supper decided. Liz was having another go at being a vegetarian so she'd have to have some kind of non-meat roast. Except, of course, that she might not be at home by then and, if she was, might no longer be a vegetarian.

Nick was a chocoholic; there was a specially rich chocolate cake that she always liked to have ready for him. She hunted in the dresser drawer for the recipe which she eventually found on a thumb-marked and greasy piece of paper in an old recipe book. She might as well make the birthday cake for Ma, as she always called Duncan's mother, at the same time, she thought, looking out the fruit cake recipe.

Liz wasn't a chocolate eater. She'd rather have a light Victoria sponge with fruit in the middle. Not even in their likes and dislikes about food were they the same. In fact, she thought, as she beat butter and sugar together, never were twins less alike in every way. In looks, Liz was small and dark, Nick tall and fair. She was fierce and quick on the draw, he was tolerant and laid back. She was highly academic and easily did well at school. He was practical and found lessons hard. She was impatient, frustrated by any small difficulty, he was tolerant and a plodder.

It was very odd, she thought as she greased the tins, that two children inheriting the same genes and brought up in the same way – not of course that you can be sure that they are, but at least with the same values – could turn out so different. No wonder they'd fought from the start. When they were little, she remembered with a smile now, she used to put them into a big round bouncer, which she and Duncan called the dog basket; it was shaped like one, but was padded and soft. They would roll around in it, crawling over each other like a pair of puppies. Soon they began to punch and wrestle in an amicable way, Liz usually winning because she was less scrupulous than her bigger brother.

She still had that great round bouncy thing somewhere. In the attic probably. She must clear out the attic one day, she resolved, putting the chocolate cake in the oven and starting to weigh out fruit. It would be nice to see again that old bouncer in which they'd biffed, and occasionally bitten, each other. Nick could easily have wrought some damage on his much smaller sister, but he never did, even when she provoked him.

As they grew older the fights were more verbal, with Liz still winning most of the battles because she was sharp and quick of speech. Nick's greatest strength, she realised now, as she cracked eggs on the side of the bowl, was that he really didn't care. She hadn't thought of that before. His sister's barbs simply bounced off him. Which was, of course, infuriating for Liz.

Against the outside world they were united; that was something which pleased Flora now as much as it had done when they were children. To attack either of them was to bring down the wrath of the other. She soon learned that if she couldn't stand their quarelling any longer, the best way was to be cross with one of them, which always made the other rush to the defence, calling her unfair. It was more peaceful to have them united against her than to have them scrapping with each other.

It was the same now that they were grown up. They squabbled, but in time of woe she could be sure that they would stand united.

Liz was ten minutes older than Nick and when they were younger used to end arguments by claiming seniority. In fact people always thought Liz was Nick's elder sister. She was old for her years, Flora reflected now, as she began washing up the cooking things, and had for a long time shared the interests of adults. Nick was still mainly interested in schoolboy things. There was something naive about him and certainly with his floppy blond hair and fair skin, he looked much younger than his years, much more than ten minutes younger than his sister.

She took the chocolate cake out of the oven, put the fruit cake in its place, made some coffee and took it out for Duncan. Nick was coming home on Thursday and it was time the day got going.

Four

"Where's Liz?" Duncan asked that evening as he handed Flora a glass of wine.

"In the shower, freshening up before she goes out."

"I shouldn't have thought that a day lying in a hammock put her in great need of freshening up."

Flora laughed.

"Spoken with all the self-righteousness of a man who has spent the afternoon cutting grass and trimming edges," she said, smiling as she raised her glass to him.

"Well, if you have a garden it has to be kept tidy," he pointed out in unnecessary justification. "And you have to admit it looks pretty good."

He stood beside her as she lay on the couch by the french windows, both of them looking approvingly down the garden, and she knew that he was feeling that special satisfaction that comes from seeing the results of hard physical work and makes even the backache seem worthwhile.

She always turned the couch round to face the window when the spring arrived, so that they could sit in the evening and see the garden change, see the first snowdrops along the front of the herbaceous bed, then the crocuses, yellow and purple, under the beech tree. And now there were late daffodils and cherry blossom and the forecast was for more warm weather tomorrow and Nick would be home on Thursday. Life was good.

"Will Liz be in for supper?" Duncan asked.

"I doubt it."

"Silly girl. Something smells pretty good in the kitchen and I must say I'm starving."

"It won't be long," she told him, finishing her wine and getting up off the couch. "I've only got to add some more vegetables to the stew."

"I'll come with you," he said, following her into the kitchen. "I want to see what that plumber got up to yesterday."

"The one from the water company? Oh, I meant to tell you. He couldn't find where our supply comes off the main, so he had to fix the meter under the sink."

"Damned nuisance."

"Yes, it was awkward for him. He was a huge Irishman and it looked so funny, his great backside bulging out between the two little doors of the cupboard under the sink," she said, laughing as she remembered. "He was such a nice man," she went on, as she took the stew out of the oven and stirred some frozen peas into it. "He'd got four strapping lads and a pregnant wife and was terrified she'd have a girl. His boys, he said, could fend for themselves, even the two-year-old could use his fists if need be, but a girl—"

"Flora."

"Yes?"

"He only came to fit a meter."

"So?"

"So why did you have to extract his life story from him?"

"I didn't. He just told me, the way people do if they come to do a job in the house."

"Not me, they don't. What I really meant was that it's a damned nuisance having to have a meter in the first place."

"We've no option, since we have a sprinkler."

"It's not as if we use it much anyway," Duncan grumbled, kneeling down and peering into the cupboard under the sink. "Can't see a thing in here."

"I'll get you the torch."

It was a big red torch which she kept in the study cupboard, next to her father's ashes.

"This year I really will do something about them," she resolved, as she took the torch back into the kitchen, handed it to Duncan and began mashing the potatoes.

Her father, so undemanding in his life, had left a request that she should scatter his ashes on White Horse Hill in Wiltshire.

"Be careful not to stand downwind of me, my dear," he had advised in a note. "It's always a bit wild up there."

She'd gone to Wiltshire to reconnoitre, leaving him behind in his urn in the cupboard of the tiny basement flat she was living in then, all she could afford on her teacher's salary. She realised immediately what he meant. It was blowing a gale up on the hill, despite being merely breezy down in the valley.

The next time she went, she took him with her, but it was Easter and the hill was swarming with people, families flying kites, children chasing each other, lovers walking hand in hand. She couldn't bring herself to do her scattering in front of such an audience.

She'd tried again the following autumn. The morning was bright and calm in Surrey, but by the time she reached her destination, a steady rain was falling and the mist on the hill merged with the heavy clouds overhead. She knew she shouldn't scatter her father's ashes on such a miserable day; his life had been sad enough without having such a dreary committal to mark its end. She wanted it to be a perfect day for him, clear and bright and preferably still. And peaceful with nobody about. There didn't seem to be many days like that on White Horse Hill. The bright days were windy and the still days were grey and dreary and too sadly apt.

She was glad that she had never added to his sorrows by telling him about her mother and David. He knew of course that Anita was living with a much younger man but he didn't know that that young man might have been his son-in-law. There seemed no point in telling him. She had never spoken to anyone else about her mother anyway; David had been her only confidant. She was glad of it now; there had been times when she had been tempted to howl on her father's shoulder.

So the months had passed, and then the years and, apart from a few unsuccessful sorties to the hill, her father's ashes had stayed in cupboards, moving with them from house to house until they settled here, in this house and garden which for fifteen years she had loved and cherished.

The scattering had not been his only request.

"Please break the news of my death to your mother yourself, Flora," he had written in the note he left for her. "Don't telephone. Go in person. Despite all, it's bound to be rather a shock for her."

She hadn't seen her mother for three years but she knew that she had moved to a service flat in Belgravia after David had left her to marry a magazine proprietor's daughter. It was to that flat that she made her way on a bleak November morning to carry out her father's last request.

At just after nine o'clock she rang the security bell and her mother's voice bade her enter.

Anita Montrose was immaculately dressed and made up ready for work. Her lips, her daughter noticed, were outlined in deep mauve, the rest filled in with a paler shade of the same colour, as if she had been reading the beauty pages in one of the magazines for which she wrote articles of consuming interest to women.

"I can see you have something to tell me," she greeted Flora brightly, almost coquettishly. "Engaged, my dear? Pregnant? Coffee while we talk?"

Oh yes, she was far too sophisticated, too much in control, to refer to the fact that this was the first time they had spoken to each other in three years or to show any surprise at her daughter's unheralded visit.

She refused the coffee and sat down, suddenly unable to find the right words. How could she phrase it? *My father is dead. David Sutton, literary agent, is no more. Your ex-husband died last night?*

Finally she came out with, "It's David. He's dead."

Nothing could have prepared her for her mother's reaction. The carefully outlined mouth opened wide in a silent scream, the eyes, under the pencilled arched eyebrows, dilated with horror and disbelief, the hands jerked up, the red-tipped fingers rigid in front of her face.

Suddenly she relaxed and rounded angrily on her daughter. "I don't believe you," she said. "Only last week, only—"

"It's true."

"He wasn't ill."

"He killed himself. Overdose. Plastic bag."

"Oh, my God. Not because of me?"

"Possibly. He always loved you."

The look she gave her daughter was one of pure gratitude, as if at some unexpected gift. But it was only a flash, a fleeting interval of mistaken sunshine in the storm. Then, clenching and unclenching her fists, her shoulders rounded, her head down, as if hugging some terrible secret, she began to sob. At last she raised her head and, lips drawn back in an animal grimace, she said in a voice that was almost a howl, "How was it *allowed?*"

The word came out as a single, long drawn out syllable.

"Where were they all? Where was that wretched wife of his?"

Had her mother heard some silly false rumour about him?

"Wife? Daddy hadn't got a wife."

"*Daddy?*" her mother repeated, staring. Then she went on, enunciating very carefully, "Flora, are you talking about David Sutton?"

She nodded, mute.

Her mother began to laugh. She flung herself back on the couch as loud, wild screams of laughter, mirthless and hysterical, seemed to fill the room.

"Oh, my God, *him.* And I thought you meant – oh, my God," she kept repeating, shuddering.

Gradually the gasping became more subdued and she sat with her head in her hands, rocking herself from side to side.

41

"Oh, this calls for a celebration. Get me a drink, Flora."

But Flora was already leaving.

She could remember it still, the feel of the brass knob under her hand as, stiffly, it turned and she let herself out into the sanity of the outside world.

"Why did the plumber make a hole in the wall?" Duncan was asking, evidently not for the first time. It sounded like a riddle of the Why-did-the-hen-cross-the-road variety.

"Oh, sorry. What?"

"You were miles away."

"I'm sorry, I was thinking about something else. Yes, he said he had to make a hole to put a lead through to an outside pad for reading the meter."

"Since they can't get to the outside without coming through the kitchen, they might as well read it in here."

"I told him that, but he said orders were orders."

"I'll just go and look outside."

"Well, don't be long. Supper's just about ready."

He was quickly back, very cross.

"He's drilled through the downpipe."

"Yes, I know, he did apologise about it, but he said it was only a little hole and the water would be coming out anyway into the drain a bit lower down. It's just that now some of it will come out a bit sooner."

"My God, Flora, he should have measured where the drill would go on the outside. You shouldn't have let him get away with it."

"Well, you know, he was so worried about his family and it *is* only a very small hole."

Duncan took a different view. He expected tradesmen to be as meticulous in their work as he was.

"Where's their number?"

"On the bills, I expect. Here. Look. And it says their lines are open for another half hour. But we don't want to get him into trouble, Duncan. He was a really nice man."

"Being nice has nothing to do with it," he told her as he dialled. "He's damaged our downpipe."

"This is the West Surrey Water Company," the recorded voice intoned. "Please press star."

He pressed star.

"If you have a query about your bill, press One."

"I don't have a query about my bloody bill," he told the voice.

"They can't hear you," Flora pointed out. "And it won't record what you say."

"If you would like to know more about our house insurance scheme, press Two," the dulcet voice invited.

"I have a perfectly good insurance scheme and if I hadn't I wouldn't come to your lot for one," he told it.

"They can't hear you, Duncan."

"If you are interested in having a water meter, press Three."

"It's the damned meter that's causing the problem."

"If you have any other enquiry, please hold."

The voice was replaced by Greensleeves.

"If I wanted to hear bloody Greensleeves, I'd play my own tape of it," he shouted as he put down the receiver.

"Temper, temper," Liz reprimanded, coming into the kitchen.

Flora gave her a reproving look. She was sorry for Duncan, usually so tolerant but always exasperated by inefficiency. Already he was looking rather sheepish; with luck he'd have forgotten all about it tomorrow and would meanwhile feel better for expressing his wrath.

"Have some supper before you go, Liz?"

"No, thanks. I'm not hungry after that huge tea. Jasper will probably take me out for dinner somewhere."

"What, in those shorts?"

"They're not shorts, Dad. They're culottes."

"You could have fooled me."

"Enjoy yourself, darling."

"Thanks, Mum."

She hugged her mother, bestowed a brief kiss on her father's head as he sat down at the table, and was off.

"I suppose," he said hopefully after she'd gone, "she might come back here after they've had dinner?"

"I doubt it. It'll be late and it's probably more sensible to stay the night."

"Sensible! That's not what we used to call it," Duncan snorted.

Five

Liz let herself into Jasper's kitchen. He had taken the front door key and left her the back. After her parents' wholesome house and beautiful garden, she found this grotty little terrace pad, with its rubbish-filled back yard, refreshingly sordid. She prowled around the untidy kitchen, stepping carefully over books and papers that were scattered across the floor, and then began pushing dirty dishes around in a bowlful of tepid water with a slightly dirtier mop, before lifting them out and leaving them to dry, streaky and not very clean, on the draining board.

Having made this gesture towards domesticity she went upstairs and lay down on the unmade double bed that almost filled the bedroom, which, with the small boxroom, constituted the first floor of the house.

Jasper wouldn't be back for at least an hour, then they would make love and go out for a pizza or maybe not, depending on how they felt. Just not to plan was joy unlimited. It seemed to her that for years and years she'd lived by parental regulations and now it was not just her pleasure but her bounden duty to break every possible rule. It was excitingly wicked to be having this affair with Jasper. And she didn't feel guilty at all, just wonderfully free. The only wickeder thing would have been if he was married, but he wasn't.

The only thing she ever felt guilty about, she thought as she lay and made patterns out of the cracks in the lath and plaster ceiling, was leaving her adolescent self in the lurch. She could still remember so clearly how she had felt in her early teens. It

45

was a different world out there, quite separate from the adult world and she'd vowed she'd never forget what it was like, she'd never join the grown-up world with its hypocrisies and boring conventions and obsession with material things.

For years they'd been in charge of her life, those adults, particularly her mother. She'd not thought about it when she was really little, but with adolescence came resentment. She clearly remembered the first time she'd realised, with an unexpected little surge of power, that she could actually hurt her mother. Flora had taken her to buy a dress to go to a cousin's wedding and had told her she looked lovely in a blue one with a fitted bodice and full skirt. She'd looked in the long glass, the assistant standing by and nodding approval and saying something about how lovely with her tiny waist and blue eyes. She'd pulled a face and said, "Yuk, it's the sort of *pretty* thing you'd wear, Mum."

It had been gratifying, the way the assistant had looked disapproving and the way her mother had winced not just at the unkindness of the remark but also that the assistant clearly thought she was a nasty, badly brought up girl. Her mother always wanted other people to like her children. Being unpleasant was a way of getting at her. The maddening thing about her mother was that she wasn't easy to get at. She had a way of listening sympathetically, of looking and being tolerant which was hard to bear.

They'd been lonely years, when she felt nobody understood what she felt like. Then, when she was fourteen, she'd fallen in love with Paul and kept her secret to herself because her love was pure and she didn't want it sullied by her friends making suggestive remarks or the adult world thinking it amusing or having anything in common with their disgusting love affairs. From a distance she'd pined for him, this unattainable sixth former.

He was tall and remote-looking and took the same bus home as she did, but got off at a later stop, so she took to getting off there too, which required telling complicated lies.

Sometimes he called in at the newsagent to collect the evening paper, so she would happen to call in too and buy sweets or one of their dreadful birthday cards which she had to tear up when she got home. She ached with love for him, but it was romantic, unrequited love; just writing his name gave her a thrill of pleasure and she spent hours trying to express her love in sonnet form. For two terms he so filled her thoughts that she nearly failed her exams.

Suddenly it was in the papers; he'd been carrying on with one of the women on the staff at his school, an elderly art mistress of twenty-six, whose husband was petitioning for divorce. *Carrying on*, that's what the paper said. How unspeakable it sounded. He'd rejected her pure, selfless love for the sordid passion of this Jezebel. She never forgave him.

Of course, she was older and wiser now, she thought, with the superior knowledge of her eighteen years. She'd grown up, had her year out, met Jasper, was on her way to college in October. Yet all the same, she did sometimes remember those adolescent vows not to forget what it felt like to be in limbo, and wanted to stretch out her hand to those who still inhabited that world.

Jasper would be back soon. She undressed, thinking it would be nice for him to come into the bedroom and, fully dressed, embrace her naked self. Nice for her too, of course, she thought as she snuggled down under the duvet, as they would after love-making. They always talked a lot afterwards; he liked to hear her talk about her childhood and her family, maybe because he'd read psychology. "Why did you feel that?" he'd ask and she'd poke around in her past and come up with all sorts of things she'd never thought of before. Practically every problem she'd ever had, she now discovered, could be traced back to some parental lapse or misjudgement. Probably they'd damaged her by doing things when she was too young to remember, like having her christened or sending her to the wrong playgroup.

She was beginning to get cold. These bright spring days

brought frosty nights. Jasper was at least two hours late. She got up and found a sweater in a drawer and was putting it on when the telephone rang. He was still in Switzerland.

"Shan't be able to get away until tomorrow," he said.

"Oh Jasper, and I've been waiting here since seven o'clock."

"Well, I did tell you I mightn't be back. I didn't realise you'd be waiting."

Of course she'd be waiting. He should have realised.

"You can stay the night," he said before he rang off.

"Mm. I'll see."

Suddenly it seemed not just cold but rather creepy, here on her own. She'd never spent a night alone here, or anywhere else come to that.

She rang home.

"Mum?"

"Yes, darling?"

"I'm at Jasper's. He's not coming back tonight. So I'm on my own."

There was a pause, then, "Do you want to come home?"

"Well, if you'd like me to. You'd have to come and get me though. The last bus went ages ago."

"That's all right. I'll be on my way in a few minutes."

"See you."

"I'm sorry Jasper wasn't back," Flora said as they drove home. "That was disappointing for you."

"Oh, I don't care," Liz told her. "I could have stayed at the house, but I thought you'd rather I came home."

"Do you want to come with us to Grandma Maltby's birthday next weekend? You don't have to, you know, she'll understand."

"Oh, I'll come. And I'll have to come back home on Friday anyway because I can't stay with Jane in London after Thursday when she's off to Brazil. Besides, Nick'll be back and I haven't seen him for yonks."

It was a very clear, starry night, the road bright in the

moonlight and the trees wraithlike in the background. They were silent for a while, then Flora said, "Your father won't be able to come. He's too much work on."

"But it's *his* mum. He *ought* to come."

"Oh, she'll understand. She'll be pleased to see you and Nick. Maybe Dad'll get up later when things aren't so hectic at work. After all it's only her seventy-fifth. We'll pull out all the stops for her eightieth."

"Unless she's kicked the bucket by then. Or maybe in her case we should say hung up her pinny?"

Flora, who would have preferred neither expression, didn't reply.

"Can I drive us up? I've hardly had any practice since I passed my test."

"Yes, if you go carefully."

"I knew you'd say that. I just *knew*. You're so predictable."

Her mother only laughed for it seemed to her that predictability wasn't such a bad quality for a mother to have.

Six

Duncan saw them off on Saturday morning, his daughter driving, Flora in the passenger seat and his six-foot-four-inches-tall son coiled up in the back.

"If she's driving," Nick said, "I'm going to stay in the life-preservation position in the back seat or, if necessary, on the floor."

"Shut up, brat," Liz said and accelerated out of the drive.

She was an aggressive driver, pushing her way in where others would have given way and ignoring blasts of the horn from other drivers. As she dodged in and out of the suburban traffic and then sped along the M25, which was remarkably quiet this Saturday morning, her mother sat alongside, knowing that comment would be counterproductive as she jammed her right foot repeatedly on to an imaginary brake in front of the passenger seat.

To drive like this and get away with it, her daughter must be a good driver, she told herself illogically, glad that they had agreed that Nick would take over for the second third of the journey and she would drive the last part up to the Dales village where Sam and Susan had long since retired.

"How about pulling in soon for a coffee?" she suggested when she felt her nerves couldn't take much more.

"Here you mean?" Liz demanded, braking sharply in order to swing the car off the road.

"Well, I didn't necessarily mean this minute," Flora said, as they came to an abrupt halt outside the windows of a Little Chef restaurant.

"Make up your mind. Do you want to stop here?"

"Yes," Nick told her, uncurling himself from the back seat where he had been lying with his arms wrapped round his head. "Never mind where, just so long as you stop." And he got out of the car, slamming the door behind him.

Flora joined him, surprised to find that her knees were literally shaking.

"How are your nerves, Mum?"

"Shattered, Nick."

"Does it matter," Liz asked, as they walked away from the car, "that I've left the keys in the ignition?"

"Matter!" Nick repeated, stopping and turning towards her. "Of course it matters, dumbo, if you've locked the car."

"I pushed down the knob by the window. I thought Mum would have a spare key. Dad gave me his."

"No, I haven't brought mine," Flora told her. "We're locked out, I'm afraid."

They each reacted in their own characteristic way.

Nick, ever the realist, looked at his watch and said, "Well, I estimate we'll be here for the next two hours."

Flora, used to keeping family spirits up, said, "Probably someone will have a key that fits and if not the AA will be here in no time."

Liz said, "Oh, shit."

Then Nick took over.

"You two go and get yourselves some coffee," he said. "No point in all three of us standing about here. I'll see if I can get help from the garage and then ring the AA. Give me the card, Mum."

So they went and sat by the window drinking coffee and watching while Nick, accompanied by a helpful garageman with a huge bunch of keys, tried to unlock the car.

"I bet they can't get one to fit," Liz said. "It's going to be an AA job. Oh, shit."

Flora was sorry for her. Liz had never found it easy to apologise. Even when they were little it was Nick who could say he was sorry and forget his offence, while Liz always refused to admit she was wrong and instead carried a burden of guilt and resentment inside her small frame for hours or even days.

The process of trying about a hundred keys was also watched by a couple sitting at the next table, a little furry animal of an old lady, bundled up in a thick woollen coat with hairy trimmings, topped by a felt-and-cardboard hat, kept in place with a kind of tubular scarf like a crocheted teacosy beneath which her wizened face peered out, her sharp little brown eyes missing nothing of what was going on outside.

"All them keys and none of them fitting," she proclaimed in the loud voice of the hard of hearing. "What are they doing, our Alan? I can't make it out at all."

"He's locked himself out, Mother. He's trying to get into his car."

"I can see that," she told him, exasperated. "What I don't understand is how did the bugger get out?"

Liz looked at her mother and they both shook with silent laughter, clutching each other's hands beneath the table.

When they recovered, Liz said, "I'm sorry about locking us out, Mum. I was stupid. I wasn't concentrating on what I was doing."

"It's all right, darling," her mother said, thinking what a healing thing laughter is, how, in the theatre or privately like this, it levels and unites. "Most of us have done it at least once. Look, Nick's just going to ring up."

Rescue came quickly. It took the AA man and two pieces of wire less than thirty seconds to break into the car. The rest of the journey was uneventful and they reached the grandparents' house by teatime.

Seven

Although her grandparents had moved ten years ago from their terrace house in Rotherham to a cottage in the Yorkshire Dales, they hardly seemed to have changed homes, Liz thought as she watched her grandmother the next day making dropped scones for tea. Of course it was different outside; there were fields and hills where there had once been streets, the bleating of sheep had replaced the noise of traffic, but inside it might have been the same house, which she remembered very well, although she had only been about eight the last time she'd visited them there. Somehow her grandmother had managed to recreate her old home, especially the kitchen where she now stood mixing the batter in the same old yellow mixing bowl. Propped up beside her was the same brown and cream Be-ro Cookery Book, for Economical Home Baking, though surely after all these years she must have known the recipe off by heart.

"Recommended by Thousands of Practical Cooks, Popular throughout the North of England," the cover proclaimed and inside it were pictures of these practical ladies wearing clothes which must have been fashionable in the nineteen thirties. Long use had weathered its pages which were burnt at the edges and had a patina which only years of contact with sugar, fat and flour, to say nothing of soft fruit and golden syrup, can bestow. The page for dropped scones was as battle-scarred as an old regimental flag.

Her grandmother carried the batter over to the cooker, which had, of course, travelled with her from Rotherham. It was a solid piece of equipment, made of cast iron, finished in mottled blue, with a rectangular griddle set in the top, which she now wiped, as she had always done, with the paper off the butter packet. When she judged the temperature was just right, she began ladling batter into the same old teacup with the cherries round the rim that she had always used.

Next she poured six little pools of the shiny yellow liquid on to the griddle; they sizzled for a moment and then rose slightly, forming tiny bubbles in the middle. At exactly the right moment her grandmother slid the fish slice under them and flipped them over. Liz had always loved to watch her perform this magic; a minute earlier and their middles would have been too runny, a minute later and they would have been over-cooked. Then when the tops and bottoms were evenly done to a pale orange-brown, each perfect circle was lifted off and deposited gently to cool on an airing tray.

They always had a proper high tea when they stayed with her grandparents. It was a substantial meal and today, being a celebration, it was a veritable carbohydrate feast of the kind their dietician daughter would not at all have approved, she thought as they sat down to eat.

"It's a pity our Daphne can't be here," Sam remarked, as if reading her thoughts. "She's away on a course."

"But she sent me a lovely card and present," Susan told them.

"What was it, Grandma?"

"It was a strange device, Liz," Sam told her, "for abstracting juice from carrots."

"I'll show it to you after. It's on the top shelf in the kitchen."

"Where it'll no doubt stay until it comes down once a year at spring cleaning."

"Oh, no, Father. I'll have a try and I'll always get it down when she visits."

"She wouldn't hold with this lot, Mother," Sam said with deep satisfaction as he surveyed the table spread with a big

white tablecloth which was weighed down with ham sandwiches, bread and butter, bowls of home-made jam and
lemon curd, an apple tart and custard pie, sausage rolls,
parkin, a jam and cream filled Victoria sponge, buttered
dropped scones and, of course, the birthday cake which
Flora had brought.

"When I retired," Sam said, cutting into his ham sandwich,
"she put us both on a diet. She said you didn't need so many
calories when you were a pensioner and less active. Do you
remember, Mother?"

"It was a very nice diet," Susan told them loyally. "There
were some of those ryvita biscuits you can buy and some fat-
free cheese which was hard to find and I remember you could
have a piece of fruit with it. And the tea couldn't have sugar
but you could take a drop of skimmed milk out of your daily
allowance."

"We used to eat the diet and then have our tea, didn't we,
Mother?"

"We enjoyed them both," she told them, beginning to shake
with laughter, "but after a bit we dropped the diet and just
managed on the rest."

When she laughed her stomach shook and took on a merrily
independent life of its own, bouncing up and down. She had
grown into a very pretty old lady, her plump, pink cheeks
unwrinkled under the thick white hair. Although fat, she was
quick on her feet and still had the slender legs and ankles that,
Flora observed, incongruously underpin many stout old parties.

"Well, what would you like to do this evening?" Susan
asked, as they sat back, bloated and slightly exhausted,
around the crumb-bestrewn table.

"You choose. It's your birthday."

"Well, Mother?"

"I always like a drive out, myself."

Flora's heart sank. She knew how Liz and Nick felt about
these outings, which involved driving their grandparents

slowly round the countryside at a speed which might have been designed to frustrate the cars behind.

"There's no hurry, not on such a lovely evening, let's enjoy the scenery," Susan would say if they exceeded thirty miles an hour, while a stream of cars was visible in the driving mirror, desperately trying to overtake.

"Road hogs," she would comment if one actually managed it.

"Why don't we drive up the dale," Flora suggested," then Liz and Nick can get out and walk and we three oldies can enjoy the scenery?"

"I'll drive, if you like," Liz offered, getting up from the table.

"No, we don't like, do we, Mum?" Nick put in before his mother could reply.

So Flora drove, her father-in-law alongside, Liz and Nick in the back with their grandmother, through the village, where they kept having to slow down to wave to friends and neighbours, then up the long, steep road towards the head of the dale. It was a clear, mild evening, the air alive with the plaintive bleating of lambs and the deeper answering call of the sheep.

She stopped half way up and parked the car by a five-barred gate into a field where a stream gushed down from the crags above. It flowed swiftly down to the lane, going under it to emerge more sedately in the marshy field at the other side whence it meandered down towards the village.

"Race you to the top," Liz said, as she and Nick got out of the car. "First up to the tree by the crag," and she was off, through the gate and tearing up the hillside.

Flora watched them. Liz had a good start and had meanly pushed the gate closed behind her. She was quick and athletic, although much smaller than her brother who, unhurried, loped along behind her, gaining gradually until he overtook her. Then she saw that he slowed down so that they reached the tree together. Such a nice nature he had, she thought, not competitive. Like his father. She wasn't sure who Liz took after, but then there are so many strands going into a child, silly just to think of the parents.

"They're a grand pair," Susan said, watching approvingly as she sat in the car.

"They love it up here, they always have, ever since you retired."

"It's a shame you can't stay longer."

"No, we must get back tomorrow. They've both got temporary jobs, you know, and then they're off abroad again. And, besides, Duncan'll be expecting us."

"And how is he, our Duncan?"

"He's fine, but very busy. He would have come, you know, of course, but he had to work this weekend."

Duncan's mother shook her head.

"It's not right. A man needs his free time with his family. I thought he was looking tired when you came up for our Mabel's funeral last month."

"Well, nobody looks their best at a funeral, Mother."

His wife was quiet for a moment, remembering the funeral of her only sister.

"Did you tell Flora about your Mabel's will?" her husband enquired.

"No, I didn't like to, but since you've raised it, maybe I should."

She turned in her seat, the better to see her daughter-in-law, and, leaning forward, said, "Our Mabel was always very fond of Duncan, having no children of her own. And you were very kind to her. She never forgot how you had her to stay after her big operation, when I couldn't have her because I was that bad with the shingles and it was enough Father could do to look after me, let alone a patient in bed."

Flora smiled, remembering Mabel as a very cheerful, entertaining old lady.

"She was no trouble," she said. "She was a lovely guest and such an easy patient. I really enjoyed having her. We laughed a lot, I remember. The children adored her."

"Well, she was very grateful to you. Now, she'd no one of her own to leave anything to and I said she wasn't to leave anything to me, which she'd planned to do, being twelve years older than I am. Father and me are quite comfortable, I told her. Our Daphne's very well paid and has no dependants and never will have as far as we can make out, living with that dog training lady like she does."

She drew breath and then went on, " 'It's the young families that need help most,' I said. 'I'd like your Duncan's family to have it,' she said. And that's what she did. We didn't say owt to him at the funeral, because it didn't seem fitting. I expect the solicitor will be writing to him."

"These things take time, Mother. The house isn't sold yet. Of course we never thought Mabel and Albert would be worth much, but it's the value of the property puts up these estates. I mean, they bought that house after the war for just over two thousand pounds."

"We thought they were daft, didn't we, Father? A great big place it was, as you know, Flora. They got it when Albert was demobbed. They said they wanted a big place because they wanted a big family and he was over thirty so they wanted to get on with it. Sad really because it never happened. Nice house in the country, big garden and just the two of them rattling around in it."

"Well, they weren't so daft because I reckon it'll fetch more than two hundred thousand now. Maybe more since that golf course's been built on their doorstep. And of course Albert left her quite a bit of money; he was clever with investments, was Albert."

"Well, it's a sad subject, both of them gone now, Father. Let's talk of something else. How's your mother, Flora. How's our Anita?"

Flora hesitated, thinking that this subject was scarcely happier than the last. She'd never let them know quite how bad things were.

"She's much the same," she said diplomatically. "Gets a bit confused, you know, and forgetful."

"Well, we all do that. I'm for ever going upstairs to get something, then I can't think what, and I only remember when I've gone downstairs again. And I put things down and can't find them. I'm always losing my spectacles. And the other day I looked everywhere for the dishcloth and found it in a flower vase on top of the cupboard. You can't get away from it, old age makes us forgetful."

"You worry too much, Mother," her husband told her. "I look at it like this. You watch a little lad or lass going to school. At the last moment they'll say, 'Oh, I forgot, we were to take some string to school, and some flowers and an elastic band,' or 'I forgot to ask you for some money for a collection,' or somesuch. They don't stand there worriting and saying, 'Oh, I've forgotten again. It's because I'm five years old.'"

His wife laughed.

"He's a grand one for cheering me up, is Sam. But about Anita, bring her up here sometime. The change might do her good."

"That's very kind of you," Flora said, knowing that she never would.

Eight

"Poor old Dad's still at work," Liz remarked as she swept the car up the drive, turned by the back door and observed the empty garage.

It was still light: the days were visibly lengthening now, you could see the difference every evening, Flora thought, as she got out of the car and made for the little side gate into the garden. As always, before she went indoors, she had to have a quick look round the garden, as if renewing an old acquaintance, while briefly noting any small changes that had taken place since they last met.

It was amazing the difference that only two warm days had made; the apple blossom was fully open now, leaves were appearing on the plum tree, wistaria showing more blue. The grass, she noticed, was uncut.

Nick and Liz had unloaded the car.

"I've taken your case upstairs, Mum."

"Thanks, Nick. Tea or coffee?"

"Coffee," they both said, following her into the kitchen.

There were three envelopes on the table; one addressed to each of them.

"What's all this about?" she said, picking hers up and turning it over.

"Perhaps it's money?" Liz suggested, ripping hers open.

"More likely bills," her brother told her.

The letters from Duncan were identical. "This is to let you know that I am leaving. I have moved all my belongings and shall not need to return for anything. I am not leaving an

60

address as I do not wish to be contacted. I enclose a telephone number at which messages can be left for me in an emergency."

Flora's letter had an extra two lines saying that he had closed their joint account and had arranged for an unspecified sum of money to be paid into a separate account in her name.

They stood motionless. It's like when the music stopped in a game of musical statues when we were little, Liz thought. Everyone transfixed, staring.

Then Flora sat down, the letter still in her hand and Nick said, "Can it be some sort of joke?" and the spell was broken.

"I'll go and look," Flora said, getting up again.

She seemed to have to push herself across the hall and up the stairs. It was as if the mechanics of her body had ceased to function efficiently, each limb had to be told what to do. But she needed to go upstairs, see if he had really taken his clothes and gone. And it was more than that: their bedroom had been their special room in the house, their place apart, where they had talked about everything and anything, where they had laughed together, and very occasionally quarrelled, where they had made love. She needed to know if this place had really been abandoned.

Duncan had kept all his clothes in an old-fashioned compactum, inherited from her father, which stood in the far corner of the room. She walked slowly across to it, reached out for the handle as she had done so many times. Even as she did so she realised that it felt too light to the touch. She heard the clang of empty coathangers; all the suits and jackets had gone. The shelves, where she had for years placed freshly ironed vests and pants, shirts and hankies, were bare, drawers were empty of sweaters and socks. There were no shoes on the racks at the bottom of the cupboard. Glancing round, she saw that his slippers had gone from his side of the bed.

So it was true, she told herself, sinking down on to the bed. But why? Could he have had some kind of brainstorm? But there had been nothing strange in his behaviour, apart from working late so often and at weekends. Apart from *what*? a cynical voice that was not her own seemed to interrupt her to ask.

Working late, working at weekends, she answered defensively. Of course that was what he'd been doing. Of course he couldn't have been with someone else.

Or could he? Other wives had been deceived. Why should she be exempt? But why this crazy behaviour with the letters? Guilt. Guilt makes people behave badly. Other people. Not Duncan. It was just so out of character. He wasn't a ladies' man. Never had been. Besides, she'd have known, she'd have been bound to notice something was wrong. They'd lived together for over twenty years. She knew him better than anyone else did. She would have known, she'd have felt it in her bones, if he was having an affair.

Or would she?

Could he have been involved in some crime, could he be running from the police? Or spying? But he wouldn't have taken all his clothes. Clothes wouldn't have been a priority.

She seemed to be trying to explain the behaviour of a stranger. It was all theoretical, not about her and Duncan at all. Who to turn to in such an emergency? For a mad moment she thought of dialling 999 for help. It passed, but still she sat with her head in her hands, utterly confused.

The door opened quietly. Nick and Liz came in. They sat on the bed one each side of her. Nobody knew what to say. It was like an inexplicable sudden death. *Why?* they were all asking themselves. She knew that Liz and Nick must be thinking that she knew more than they did. She could see it in their faces.

"I don't know either," she said and began to weep.

They both reached out to her, both held her, the three of them rocking together.

"We'll have to find out more tomorrow," Nick said, when she was calmer. "I'll ring that number for you, shall I?"

"Oh, I don't know. I don't know what to think."

"Well, I think you need a good solicitor," Liz said, echoing something she'd once heard somebody say in similar circumstances.

"Oh, no. I don't want to do anything that might make things worse by getting all legal. It may just be a passing madness and he'll come back. I don't want to close doors."

"All right. Let's sleep on it," Nick said.

"Or rather lie awake on it," Liz corrected him.

Flora remembered something.

"I have to go to collect Gran tonight," she told them.

"Oh, no, tell them you can't have her back until next week."

She sighed and shook her head.

"No, Liz. I can't do that. I promised I'd go tonight. They need the room."

"We'll come with you. At least we can keep her distracted."

"Thank you, that would be a great help."

She was aware, as she stood up, that she felt very old and stiff, as if she'd been in bed for months. In a daze, she began putting her things together in the disorientated way of a convalescent leaving hospital, gathering together possessions long unused but required now for the return to the outside world.

"I'll drive," Nick said. "And I think you should have a brandy before we go. I'll go and get you some."

She didn't like it, but forced it down, grimacing at the fiery taste of it. Then they all went back to the car, which was still warm from their long drive home from the north. It seemed an age ago, a different life. Was it really only yesterday evening that they were driving up the dale with the grandparents, that she'd watched Liz and Nick racing up the hillside and felt so pleased with them, so happy with her family?

And all the time Duncan had been here methodically emptying cupboards, writing notes, addressing envelopes. Or perhaps he had started the minute they drove off, perhaps all the time they'd been packing the car with cases and presents and the big tin which held his mother's birthday cake, he'd been longing for them to go, rejoicing as he waved them off that now at last he'd be able to get on with his urgent tasks.

Had he been relieved to see the back of them, his wife and children? She tried to remember how he'd looked, wracked her memory for any little signs of difference in him that she hadn't noticed at the time, but which the more knowing eye of hindsight might now perceive. But there was nothing, nothing at all.

It was dark now; she stared blankly out into the night, observing the familiar route to the home, which they'd travelled so often over the past year and would no doubt travel many times more because life must go on, just as it must go on when a loved one dies.

Nine

"Where's that man gone?" her mother enquired after Flora had given her breakfast and helped her to dress. "Not sight nor sign of him last night. You know, that man you used to have hanging about here."

"He's working," Flora told her. "I've a lot to do today, Mother, so I'll leave you now. Mrs Herbert will be in soon and said she'd keep you company for a while. I've put the cards out for patience."

"You're always too busy, that's your trouble. Rushing to do everything at once. You should do things peace mince."

"Peace mince?"

"You know, pie meal."

"Oh yes, piecemeal. Well, don't you worry about that, just enjoy your patience."

"And don't you worry either, so there," her mother replied.

A door linked her sitting room with their landing, but the flat had its own staircase up from their kitchen. It was down these stairs that Flora went now to clear the breakfast away before she made herself ring the number that Duncan had given them in his note.

It was an old-fashioned kitchen. She'd never wanted the modern sort with everything hidden behind matching doors so you couldn't tell where the refrigerator was. Hers had various unmatching cupboards and cabinets acquired over the years as they accumulated more things to put in them. An elderly couch leant against one wall and a Welsh dresser against another. A big pendulum clock ticked loudly on the wall above the cooker, while up aloft herbs and dried flowers hung in bunches from an old-fashioned clothes airer.

In the middle of the kitchen was the big table which always seemed to her to be the centre of the house. Around it they had sat for countless family meals, on it she had baked and the children had painted and Duncan had done odd bits of carpentry. When the children came in from school they had rushed to it, often with friends in tow, and had sat there eating home-made bread and cakes, telling indignant tales of the injustices meted out to them during the day.

When they were little they did their homework at this same table, while she cleared the dishes and began cooking the supper, as quietly as she could, although frequently interrupted with calls for help. Later, of course, they went up to their rooms to study and she could indulge in the luxury of listening undisturbed to the radio while she cooked or ironed.

Yes, it had always been a warm and welcoming kitchen, but today it felt strangely hostile, as she stood there at the bottom of the stairs. It seemed to her, in her overwrought state, that it was blaming her. What had all this domesticity led to? Where had she gone wrong? Why should a fundamentally kind and decent, hardworking man like Duncan treat her like this if she didn't deserve it?

She hardly dared admit to herself that she felt this guilt. She knew that if she breathed so much as a suspicion of it to anyone else, they'd think she was mad or, worse still, feeble and wimpish. But for such a man to disown his own family, apparently not care if he never saw his wife or children again, after all these years of caring and sharing, of loving and home-making, it didn't make sense unless something had driven him to desperation. Where had she gone wrong?

Stop it, Flora. Just ring that number.

She couldn't find the piece of paper with the number on. She begun hunting in the kitchen litter bin, then in waste paper baskets around the house, getting more and more frantic, more appalled at her own carelessness. Probably Nick and Liz still had theirs, but Nick had gone to his shelf-filling job at the superstore and Liz had gone to see Jasper. She'd encouraged her to go; it might help her to talk to him, an older man. Besides, she didn't want to ask them for the number, admit her own inefficiency.

She made herself sit down and go through her actions last night. She'd still had her coat on when they went into the kitchen and saw those envelopes. She went and looked in her wardrobe; the paper was in her coat pocket.

Her hand shook as she dialled the number. The voice on the answerphone was Duncan's voice, sounding just the same as he always did, there on the other end of the line. Though of course he wasn't actually on the other end of the line, he'd recorded this message in some unknown room while they were in Yorkshire.

She hadn't expected to hear his voice. She didn't know what she'd expected, but not that, not her husband sounding so normal. She couldn't speak after the tone, although he was telling her to. She put the receiver down and went out into the garden.

This was always her place of healing, she thought as she sat on the old bench by the espalier pear trees and looked down at her garden, waiting for it to perform its magic, but there was no warm response, no lifting of the spirit. How heartless it all seemed, just going on, springlike and uncaring.

Suddenly she wondered how she'd manage it on her own. The grass looked frighteningly long; at this time of the year it never seemed to stop growing. Duncan was the only one in the family who could manage the old Atco mower; she couldn't even get it out of the shed and Nick, though strong enough, didn't have Duncan's skill in managing the vagaries of the machine. Besides, he'd be away next month. And all the other heavy jobs which had been Duncan's, what of them? As she looked, the garden ceased to be a garden any more and became just a collection of anxieties, of tasks she couldn't cope with now because, like everything else in their marriage, it had been shared. She couldn't bear to look at it.

She went back indoors. The silence in the house was tangible. When the telephone rang it seemed to split the silence like a gunshot.

It was Duncan's secretary.

"Sorry to bother you, Mrs Maltby," she said, "when Mr Maltby is having his week's holiday, but I wonder if I could have a word with him, just very briefly? I need to ask him something."

"Ask him something?"

"Yes. It's just that there's a company I'm to ring and I haven't got the name of the gentleman I'm to contact. I think your husband would remember it."

"He isn't here. I mean he's gone out."

"Oh, then don't worry. I can probably trace the name and if not, I'll just ring the company and they'll help me, I'm sure."

"I'm sure," Flora said and then realised she was repeating last words, the way the elderly and confused sometimes do.

"I'll get on to them now. I'm sorry to have troubled you. Enjoy your holiday."

"Thank you."

So he'd told them at the office last week that he'd be away. It was all prearranged. As he'd lain dozing in the garden last weekend, he'd had it all planned. Perhaps he hadn't been asleep, just pretending as he lay there working it all out. Was he smiling to himself as he watched, through half-closed eyes, his unwitting wife and daughter, she thought with sudden anger. Yes, now she did feel anger. Cling to it, she thought, it's better than guilt.

Someone came in the front door. It was Liz. Pale and wretched, she stumbled into the kitchen towards her mother.

"Oh, Mum," she said, and burst into tears.

"Come here," Flora said, drawing her to the couch and sitting down beside her, her arms around her, forgetting all her own woes in concern for her daughter's uncharacteristic collapse. Liz, always so strong and confident, how fragile, how slight, she felt now as she sobbed in her mother's arms.

"I'm sorry, Mum. I'm sorry."

"Hush, there's nothing to be sorry about, my darling."

"But I'm not being any help to you. I'm useless."

"Of course you're helping. It's just that we're all in a state of shock, that's all."

"And look, I've made you cry too," Liz said, managing a damp little smile.

"No harm in tears. Nature's way of helping us to relax," Flora told her, dabbing at her daughter's face and then at her own. "Now you sit here and I'll put the kettle on. We both need a cuppa."

As she filled the kettle and measured coffee into the cafe-tière, she watched her daughter slowly collecting herself.

"Jasper all right?" she asked.

Liz nodded.

"We've parted," she said. "I'll tell you about it later."

Now was not the time to tell her mother how she'd gone to Jasper, wanting to tell him all about it, but she'd been over-whelmed with the shame of it. It was so stupid, but she'd just felt so ashamed of her father and couldn't talk about what he'd done. It wasn't logical, it couldn't be analysed in the way she'd always analysed things. If she'd really trusted Jasper, she thought later, she'd have been able to tell him.

So she'd just said nothing and they'd got into bed together, but it had all gone wrong and she'd wanted to get up and go away but hadn't had the courage, so had stayed and experi-enced his love-making, just experienced it. Detached, obser-vant and finally repelled, she had not enjoyed the experience.

And he hadn't even noticed. He'd just gone on screwing. And afterwards he'd gone into his usual routine of wanting her to talk about her problems and her family and her past and she'd felt furious not just with him but with herself that she had ever been so disloyal.

So everything about him had suddenly become loathsome

and she'd told him she was going. And then she'd realised that he didn't really care at all. He was just a thirty-six-year-old divorcee who had enjoyed having an affair with a girl who had only been seventeen when he deflowered her.

She couldn't tell her mother all this, not now, she thought, as for the first time in her life she put somebody else's needs before her own.

"Oh, this coffee is good," she said instead. "Thanks."

They sat in silence for a while and then she asked, "Have you made any plans, Mum? Did you ring that number?"

Flora shook her head.

"Yes, I tried. I got through but I couldn't bring myself to say anything. Sorry. But I will, I promise."

"Just do it when you're ready," Liz said gently, in a voice which Flora recognised as her own. "Don't force yourself."

"Thanks, darling. But of course I must do it soon, find out what's going on, I mean. I don't even know where he is."

"Yes, I find that's the worst bit, not knowing where my own father is. I mean I know he was away a lot recently, but we did know where he was and why."

Did we, I wonder, her mother thought, but didn't say.

"Mum," Liz said suddenly. "What about ringing Milly Chatterton? She always knows everything about everyone in the firm and she lives quite near now, doesn't she?"

"Oh, darling, not her! Not old Chatterbox."

This was the nickname they had always given to the wife of Bob Chatterton, a colleague of Duncan's at Prescotts. She was one of those kind-hearted but rather silly women, Flora thought, that it's as well not to get too involved with.

"We're acquaintances, of course," she went on, "but hardly close friends."

The thought of asking loquacious Milly for information about Duncan appalled her.

"You wouldn't need to ask her in cold blood, just happen to drop in on her when you're passing. All right, you're not close friends, but you do know her quite well."

How well do you have to know someone before you can ask them for the whereabouts of your husband? It was a question of etiquette that hadn't arisen in her life hitherto.

The telephone rang at the other end of the kitchen. Liz signalled to her mother to stay put and went to answer it.

"Just a minute, I'll see if she's around," she said.

She covered the receiver with a cushion and came back to her mother.

"Speak of the devil," she whispered in her ear.

"Not Duncan?"

"No. Milly. I can say you must have gone out."

"No, I'll take it."

"Flora, is that you?" the familiar, rather breathless voice asked. "Look I happen to be passing your door on the way to see Mary. You know Mary Fowler? Well, she's just had this baby and she's in the Barford Road Maternity Unit. And I thought I might just call in on you on the way. Visiting's from three till five so I could come at about two, after lunch."

"That's fine. We'll have coffee in the garden," Flora said and put the receiver down before she could change her mind, before she could be tempted to remember that she'd promised to go out this afternoon or any other excuse not to have to listen to Milly. Apart from anything else, she always found Milly exhausting. You'd think that people who never stop talking would be restful to entertain, because you don't need to think of anything to say, but they're not, they wear you out, drain you utterly.

"Well done, Mum," Liz said. "Look, you cook something for lunch and I'll take mine up and have it with Gran, then you can have a quiet spell before the Chatterbox's visitation."

"Thanks, darling. I thought we'd just have omelettes. Goodness, it's nearly one o'clock, I'd better get on with it."

She turned away quickly to hide the tears which seemed to come easily now at any little show of kindness.

*　　*　　*

71

At exactly two o'clock the car drove up and Milly Chatterton rang the front door bell. She was a tall, well built woman, red of cheek and dark of hair, with large brown eyes and a big mouth which had that elastic look that seems to go with garrulity.

"Well, here I am," she said, "on the dot. I hope you don't mind, but it was on my way and I haven't seen you for simply ages."

"Of course, I don't mind. Come along in. Coffee's ready and I thought we'd have it outside."

"Oh yes, it's a shame to be indoors on such a lovely day," Milly began, following her out to the patio and settling herself down at the table. "Yes, this is Mary's fifth, would you believe? That makes five babies she's had in under seven years. They're Roman Catholic, of course. Don't get me wrong, I've nothing against Roman Catholics, but when you think of all the money they get in child allowances, it doesn't seem right, does it?"

She paused to take the cup which Flora was offering her, sniffed and exclaimed, "Oh, what a good smell the coffee has, the real thing, isn't it? I must admit I never have anything but Instant at home, but you can tell the difference, can't you? No thanks, no sugar. But I must say she looks after them all beautifully, Mary does, though how she manages I can't think. I suppose it helps having two grannies in good working order. I never got much help that way myself, though my sister did babysit now and then. Mind you, child allowances were nothing like they are now, were they, in our day?"

She drew breath, looked briefly around her and went on, "Your garden's looking a picture. It would scare me, having a garden this size, I must say, but of course it's lovely in the summer. Bobby isn't very keen on gardening. I mean he does it, don't get me wrong, but he'd rather be on the golf course any day. He doesn't mind cutting the lawn, men don't, do they? It's just the messing around with plants and suchlike that

72

he doesn't care for. It must take Duncan half the weekend to cut this lot though. How is he, by the way?"

She knows, Flora thought, she knows he's gone. It's no good prevaricating. In the end it'll be less humiliating just to come out with it.

"He's gone," she said. "He has left us. This weekend."

"I'm so sorry," Milly said and her eyes, Flora saw with surprise, filled with tears. But perhaps it wasn't so surprising for they were eyes that always registered emotion rather than the light of intelligence. Milly was a kind person; she really did care about other people in her own stupid way.

"I'd no idea he'd left you," she was saying now. "I mean I did know that something was *going on*. Don't get me wrong, I never listen to gossip, I don't hold with it, but Bobby told me in confidence that he was worried about Duncan and that woman."

"That woman?"

"Fiona from Publicity."

"Fiona from Publicity?"

She was doing it again, this inane repetition.

"You know how Prescotts subcontracted all their publicity?"

She shook her head.

"They shut down their own publicity department three years ago. Downsizing they called it. Bobby didn't hold with it. You don't get the same commitment, he said. No, I won't have another cup. Well, perhaps just a half. But anyway they did it and poor old Podders who'd done quite well for the firm for years was made redundant with the rest of them and this other company took over. Merriman and Cheer they were called, a good name for a publicity firm, don't you think?" she added, with a little laugh.

Flora nodded, not caring.

"Go on," she said, not that Milly needed any prompting.

"You remember when it was being set up, how they had that weekend conference in a lovely hotel near Stratford-on-Avon?

Well, when Bobby got back he said how well Duncan had got on with this Fiona woman. Nothing *wrong*, you understand. Didn't he mention it to you?"

"No, but I do remember Duncan talking about the conference."

"Well, then of course, they did keep coming across each other afterwards at meetings and suchlike. I mean there was that weekend conference in Brussels last April – no, I tell a lie – it must have been May because I remember Bobby came back the day before my birthday and brought me a little model of the Mannekin Pis. Rather rude, I thought it, but I had to laugh. Anyway I suppose it just happened, the way it sometimes does. And of course with Duncan being so good looking, the girls were bound to be after him, weren't they?"

Flora looked at her, startled. This was a new view of Duncan. Of course she'd always liked his face, thought it a kind, ordinary sort of face, but never up there among the handsome.

Milly caught that look of surprise and went on, "Well, I don't mean glamorous like a film star, but sort of rugged, mannish, you know. Some women just go for that sort of weatherbeaten look, don't they? And some women are very unscrupulous. Not just the young girls. I mean there seem to be so many divorcees and widows about nowadays, don't there? Offices are full of them. Not that Duncan ever seemed to notice if anyone fancied him, Bobby said, always too absorbed in his work, was Duncan."

Yes, that's how he always seemed to me, Flora thought, that's how the world saw him too, a man whose life was his work and his family. It was impossible to relate that man, who loved to talk shop with his colleagues, who loved his home and garden, which he kept so meticulously, its lawn weedless and its edges trim, to this new Duncan. They were mutually exclusive.

"I've often thought," Milly said, leaning back in her chair and looking reflectively round the garden, "that it must be quite difficult for wives of these good-looking husbands. I'm lucky really, Bobby being short and fat."

She paused and then leant forward, as if to get back to the matter in hand.

"Bobby was quite upset about this business of Duncan, I can tell you. I did keep asking him if he thought I should come and see you about it, but he said not, it wouldn't do any good and might stir things up. He hoped it was just a passing affair and least said soonest mended."

"So everyone knew about it?"

"Well, quite a few people at work. I mean people at their level, not the ones lower down, if you see what I mean. Not that I'm a snob or anything, don't get me wrong."

"Duncan's secretary didn't know. I spoke to her this morning."

"Old Edith? Oh, she wouldn't know anything. She never lifts her eyes from her desk. Edith would never pick up on any office tittle-tattle," Milly said, rather contemptuously, Flora thought, for one who had just said she didn't hold with gossip.

She was torn between wanting to pretend that of course she'd known all about it and the need to extract information. She wanted to know more about this Fiona, but couldn't bring herself to ask.

"Well, of course, as I say," Milly rattled on unprompted, "Fiona and Duncan were really thrown together. I was surprised at Duncan, but Bobby says some middle-aged men are like that. It's called the male menopause and makes them stray. You know, they suddenly think, my God, I'm getting old and I want my youth back."

"Is she very young?" Flora asked, thinking of Liz and her thirty-six-year-old lover.

"No. Well, I suppose she is by our standards. Early thirties. Divorced. A career woman. Bobby says that's partly the trouble. Men nowadays like to have a partner who's got her own career. It's a sort of status symbol, like a big car or a boat. Funny really because it used to be the other way round and men didn't like to think their wives went out to work. It undermined them. Nowadays it's great if their wives – well, partners you have to say nowadays, don't you? – earn more than they do. Well, I've never had a career, apart from a bit of secretarial in the early days, but Bobby's never strayed. Mind you, he's not a great one for sex, isn't Bobby. He'd rather have a beer any day."

She looked at her watch.

"Ooh, is that the time? I must go. But I'm really sorry, Flora, I really am. I never thought such a thing would happen to you and Duncan. I've thought of you as a really settled couple, like me and Bobby. Now, if there's anything we can do to help you, just tell us. Of course, Bobby will have to go on working with Duncan, I mean they're together almost every day. But don't get me wrong, that doesn't mean we're on his side."

"I hope it won't be a matter of taking sides."

"Of course not. Now, I must be on my way or I'll miss visiting time. They're quite strict about visiting at the Maternity. Quite right too, visitors can be very tiring when you've just had a baby. I've got a little jacket for her," she went on as they walked up towards the house, Flora steering her round to the car at the front, to avoid her having to meet Liz in the house. "They say you get a lot of presents for the first and second babies and then it gets down to a mere trickle and nobody bothers after the fourth. Not that I'd know about that. We stopped at two, like you and Duncan. But by the fifth there can't be many baby clothes to hand down, I mean everything'll be worn out, won't it?"

She was still talking as she got into the car. "What a price baby clothes are nowadays, aren't they?" she said, starting the engine and winding down the window. "I could hardly believe it. 'That's almost as much as I'd pay for a cardigan for myself,' I said to the girl. Of course, as she said, there's a lot of work in these tiny clothes, very fiddly too. Not that I minded spending the money, don't get me wrong. And I must say it's a very pretty little jacket with crochet work round the edges."

Mouthing something that Flora couldn't hear, she waved and moved a few jerky yards down the drive.

"Left the brake on, silly old me," she called out of the window, before disappearing rather more smoothly round the corner.

Liz was waiting anxiously in the kitchen.

"What did she have to say?" she asked immediately her mother came in.

Flora hesitated.

"Do you mind if we leave it till this evening, darling? We can talk better after supper, the three of us. I've Gran's tea to get now. She likes a high tea nowadays and then just a hot drink last thing. It's what they do in the home and it seems to suit her."

"I'll give you a hand," Liz said, putting her arm round her mother's waist, and resisting the temptation to question her further. "No, you lie on the couch and just tell me what to do. You look absolutely exhausted."

"Milly is very tiring," Flora admitted.

"She was here for ages. I thought she was supposed to be in a rush to get to the hospital."

"She was. I'm afraid she won't have much time to see her friend; she'll only just get there before visitors are thrown out."

"So much the better for mother and child," her daughter told her.

Ten

Flora watched through the kitchen window as Nick did battle with the lawn mower. Newly dragged out of the toolshed, the huge and ancient Atco stood like some old warhorse in the yard. It had a defiant look as it sullenly resisted all Nick's attempts to activate it. He pulled at the starter to no avail. He heaved, he tugged, he altered the choke, checked the petrol, fiddled with this and that, tugged again. She turned away, unable to bear watching her son's frustration, his fruitless expenditure of nervous energy. The Atco was a one-man machine and that one man was Duncan.

"Gran did a great demolition job on her high tea," Liz said, coming into the kitchen with a trayful of empty dishes. "Are you going to tell the other grandparents, Mum?" she asked suddenly. "Obviously Dad hasn't. Unless he sent them a charming note, like ours," she added with a bitter little smile.

It was not a look which Flora had ever seen on her daughter's face. Liz's was an expressive face, quick to show amusement or indignation, but this hurt, inward-looking bitterness she had not seen before. Already Liz was changing.

"No, darling. It would only upset them and there's nothing they can do to help. I'll wait a while. Look, why don't you go and bring Nick in for a cup of tea? He wouldn't have one when he came in from work, just shot out there to mow the lawn."

"OK. I expect he's flooded the engine by now, so it'll give the poor Atco a break."

"I'm sorry, Mum," Nick said as he sat at the table drinking

78

tea. "I don't know what gets into that Atco. I mean it's a great machine, when it gets going. It's just that it won't start."

"Why don't we simply buy another mower?" Liz asked.

"It's hardly the time to buy expensive machinery, not until we know where we stand," her mother told her.

"Well, let's just tell Dad that if he chooses to go off, he's got to provide something to cut the bloody lawn with."

"Not yet," Flora said.

"Leave it, Liz," Nick warned.

"When I get a job—"

"Mum, please, don't think about that until we're through this. You really aren't fit to go applying for jobs at the moment," Liz told her, getting up to clear the dishes. "And we can live economically until it's all sorted out."

"Just what I was thinking," her brother said. "I think it's a jolly good thing to economise. And it's good for the environment too. I mean take this water metering. We could really save on water bills. Look at you, Liz!"

"What?" she asked, startled.

"Standing there, with the tap running on to one mug. You should keep it to wash with all the others."

"It stains if I don't wash it straight away. It's because I don't have milk in my tea."

"We could have a bowl ready just for rinsing, then we could save all the washing up until night time."

"Or store them in the bath and wash them once a week?"

"All right, be sarcastic, but you know what I mean. Thank goodness we never got round to having a dishwasher. They use gallons of water. I wonder what the meter reads. Do you know, Mum?"

"I've no idea. It's just about impossible to see under there."

Nick disappeared into the cupboard under the sink.

"Yes, I get your point," his muffled voice was heard to say. "Can't see a thing."

So she went to the study to get the torch from its place in the cupboard next to her father's ashes.

"0014.15," Nick read out.

He was lying on his stomach, his long legs sticking out across the kitchen floor.

"When was it put in, Mum?"

"Last Friday week."

Was it only ten days since the fat plumber had forced his bulky self into the cupboard? And drilled a hole through the downpipe and Duncan had tried to complain to the water company and got so cross with the answerphone? Her eyes suddenly filled with tears at the thought of that other Duncan, who had so strangely vanished. She bent over the oven, pretending to check the progress of the steak and kidney pie, so that the children wouldn't see her tears.

"There must be other ways we could save water, recycling it for example," Nick was enthusing.

"Shall I save this tea in the pot for you to shave with, baby brother?"

"No, I'm serious, Liz. I mean take Gran's hot water bottle—"

"I'd rather not."

"Every night she has this bottle, yes?"

"Yes," Flora said. "She does."

"And what do you do with it in the morning?"

"I empty it into her bathroom basin."

"*Exactly!*" Nick exclaimed triumphantly. "Just wasted, when it could be recycled."

"You're not suggesting I should make her morning tea with it?"

"No, but it would do for washing in."

"But it's cold, Nick. Mum would have to tip it into the kettle to warm it up and then the kettle would make everything taste all rubbery."

"All right."

He thought for a moment.

"I know. She could put it into the lavatory cistern," he said. "It says here that every flush costs a penny. How interesting that it really does cost a penny to spend a penny, if you see what I mean."

"But the cistern's full already, you idiot."

"Well, she'd just have to flush the lav and then quickly tip the water from the bottle into the cistern before it filled up."

"By the time her arthritic fingers had taken the stopper out of the bottle the cistern would have filled itself up already."

"She could slacken it off beforehand."

"Oh, I can imagine the scene. Gran sitting there with this slackened-off stopper in her bottle, jumping up after her pee and spilling the bottle water all over the bathroom carpet. I hope you'll be around to mop up the mess."

"She'd have to be trained."

"*Trained?* And you'd do the training, I suppose. How long is it since you tried to show Gran how to do anything?"

"Well, perhaps it would be best if Mum just emptied it into a jug and left it ready by the lavatory."

"Nick, Mum has plenty to do without emptying hot water bottles into jugs, which have to be emptied into cisterns the instant Gran has had a pee."

Nick sighed.

"Maybe you're right," he conceded. "But it does seem a waste."

He went back under the sink.

"That's odd," he called back. "The meter's still going round and round. Quite fast. And we're not running any water."

"I expect it's the tank filling up."

"Ah, yes, Mum, I hadn't thought of that. There'll always be a bit of delay. Well, I think I'll go and have another try at the Atco."

"Supper will be ready in about forty minutes. I've just got the vegetables to do now."

"I'll do the spuds," Liz volunteered.

From the other window, the west-facing one by the sink, they saw Nick pushing the mower round to the top lawn. At the first pull it spluttered into life. He gave them a triumphant wave. The engine died.

"Oh, poor Nick," Flora exclaimed. "If only his father was here to show him."

"If his father was here, he wouldn't need to be shown," Liz pointed out, as she peeled the potatoes.

"Well, Nick has helped mow the lawns before," Flora told her, "but of course Duncan always set it up for him."

"He should bloody well have cut the grass before he went," Liz said. Then she laughed and went on, "Definition of a gentleman, Mum: A man who cuts the grass before deserting his wife."

Deserted wife, Flora thought. The words ran through her head. How Victorian it sounded; poor helpless little abandoned woman. She would not be put into such a category, she thought angrily. This time anger remained with her; it steeled into resolution. She walked out of the kitchen and went upstairs. From the telephone by the bed she rang the number again and this time left a message. Coldly, firmly she told him that she must speak to him, that she must know where he was and what his plans were. Only then would she decide what she would do about it. But not before she had heard from him.

Then, exhausted, she lay down on the bed. She often felt like this nowadays, suddenly and inexplicably tired. Perhaps not inexplicable, she told herself, in the circumstances to be emotionally drained. All the same, to have to lie down after the exertion of telephoning her husband was a bit pathetic, wasn't it?

Anger left her; only weariness and sadness remained, as if she was in mourning for her dead marriage, for her rejected self. Her father too had been rejected, she thought, vaguely reminiscing now. Perhaps it ran in the family. How that poor man had gone on loving and loving, without one kind word from his beloved, always hoping for the miracle that never happened. He must have clung to the memory of the few months when presumably they were happy together, when Anita had loved him. Because surely her mother must have loved him once; why else should she have married him? He'd lived on the hope that one day she would return, until the time came when even he had to recognise that all hope was gone and, unable to live without hope, had killed himself.

What a terrible, destructive thing love can be, she thought, as she lay there. I must not let the love I have for Duncan keep me hoping and pining. Dear and gentle father, let me learn a lesson from you. A lesson of self-preservation. I will not do as you did. I will not let rejected love destroy me. And by the way, I do not love my mother; I care for her out of duty and pity too, but not love. Perhaps one day my own children will feel the same about me, but they will feel it with regret and sadness, the sadness of knowing that children can never love their parents as much as their parents love them.

And that's right and proper and as it should be, she told herself, getting briskly off the bed, nature ordains it. So I shall now powder my nose and return to the kitchen and get on with life because I still have a family and a family must be fed.

Meanwhile Nick had come back into the kitchen, where his sister was pouring boiling water on to a pan of potatoes.

"How's the lawnmower from Hell?" Liz asked.

"I've given it up. It's a waste of time. I'll do the edges and some weeding instead. I'll give the chap who services it a ring and ask him to come round on Saturday and show me what I'm doing wrong."

"Will you be here?"

"Yes, I'm off at the weekend. On night shift next week."

"He'll wonder why you don't ask Dad about the mower."

"I suppose I'll just have to tell him."

"No, not yet. Mum doesn't want the whole neighbourhood talking about it. I *think* she's gone to ring that number."

"Did she say so?"

"No, but there was a look on her face. You know, when she gets determined?"

He hesitated.

"Liz," he began.

"Yes?"

"When Mum was with Gran this morning, I rang that number."

"You didn't!"

"Yes, I told him he'd hurt Mum dreadfully and he should have talked to her properly. And us too, because we're not kids any more. And I asked him what he was going to do about money. I wish now I'd added a word about the Atco."

"Nick—"

"Yes?"

"When Mum was down the garden with old Chatterbox this afternoon, I rang that number too. I left him an earful on the answerphone."

"Milly was here? Did Mum invite her?"

"No, she invited herself," Liz told him. "I reckon she spilled the beans about Dad. Mum didn't want to talk to me about it. I think she wanted to wait until we were both here."

She took the lid off the pan and prodded the potatoes.

"Don't ask her anything, Nick, please," she begged, turning to her brother. "She'll tell us all about it in her own time after supper."

"Sh, she's coming."

Their mother came into the kitchen. She was looking flushed and somehow much better.

"I've done it," she told them. "He'll find a message on the answerphone when he gets back from wherever he is."

"Oh, good. Well done, Mum," they both said, knowing, but not saying, that actually he would find three messages.

"And here's a bottle of wine. I think we all need it. It's been a long day. Could you open it, Nick?"

She handed the bottle to her son and went across to the oven. The steak and kidney pie was perfect. She took it out and put it on the side to keep warm.

Nick was watching her. He poured her a glass of wine.

"That's the cook's glass," he said, as he handed it to her, echoing, she realised, the words that Duncan had sometimes used.

"Thank you, Nick," she said, raising her glass to him and wondering if it was unconscious, the way he was taking on his father's rôle, this son of hers who was sometimes so childish. She didn't want him to have to grow up suddenly. It wasn't fair; he should be allowed to grow up in his own time, like other kids of his age.

"Your hands are filthy, Nick," Liz said.

"I know. I didn't want to waste water on them. I thought I'd save them until there was something else equally dirty to wash."

"Like your neck, you mean?"

"More like your feet."

"It's only because I go barefoot now that summer's come. It's good for your feet to go without shoes," his sister told him as she took the potatoes off the gas and prepared to strain them.

"You could wash them in that potato water. It's an awful waste just to pour it down the sink."

"Get out of the way before I pour it over your head."

Reassured by this familiar old banter, Flora sipped her wine and began laying the table, around which they would sit, as so often before, only tonight it would just be the three of them and afterwards she would tell them, as calmly as she could, the Milly version of what had happened to the absent member of their family.

Eleven

D uncan didn't reply to her message on the answerphone. Instead a letter arrived for her from his solicitor the next Saturday morning.

It was a miserably cold, wet day; the weather seemed to have given up its attempt at summer and reverted to winter. It hardly seemed possible, as they sat around the kitchen table, with the central heating full on, that they had so recently breakfasted in the garden.

"Well, what does it say, Mum?" Nick asked, reaching for another croissant and trying to sound casual.

"This Mr Gordon Bannister says that since his client – that's Duncan – doesn't wish to be in direct communication with me, would I please send him the name and address of my solicitor so that negotiations can begin."

"Do we have a solicitor?"

"No. The last time we needed one was when we bought this house."

"Oh, I thought a solicitor was the sort of thing people had, like a dentist."

"Oh, really, Nick," Liz rounded on him. "You have a dentist because you have to, for your teeth. You don't have a solicitor unless you need one. You don't just keep one like an expensive pet."

"Sh, you two. I'll have to get a solicitor, Nick, if that's the way your father wants to do things. I'll just have to go along with it."

"Can you afford it? I mean if Liz says it's an expensive pet?"

"Dad'll have to do the affording. He can't expect Mum to fork out for all his silly nonsense. If he wants to mess up all our lives he can bloody well pay for it himself."

For a moment it seemed as if she might burst into tears of rage, then she went on more calmly, "Where's he getting all the money from, Mum? I mean we've never been rich. We only just managed, didn't we? And now he's going to keep up two homes, isn't he?"

"Well, I think he'll be obliged to. I hope he will. But, as I told you last night, this Fiona from Publicity seems to be in a well-paid job."

"I wish she was in a well-lined coffin."

"Thinking like that will get us nowhere, Liz," her mother told her wearily.

"Sorry, Mum."

And she filled up her mother's coffee cup to show that she meant it.

"Didn't Gran have a solicitor?" Nick put in. "He came to the house years ago. I remember because it was half-term and she made a great fuss about giving him tea and he didn't eat it and I had all the cream cakes after he'd gone."

"It's very illuminating, the things you remember," his sister remarked.

"No, that was the finance man who sees to Gran's affairs," Flora told him. "I don't know if he was a solicitor. I rather think not. He came from her bank, as far as I remember. He has power of attorney anyway. He was a nice man, but I don't think he'd be the right one to ask about this."

"I thought Gran didn't have any money?"

Flora shrugged.

"I don't know. She must have earned a lot in her time, but she lived quite extravagantly."

"Not now, she doesn't. She lives on us."

"Liz! I imagine she was comfortably off and my father left her half of everything and his flat, which probably was worth quite a bit by the time he died. But that's beside the point.

The man you remember, Nick, wouldn't be the one to help. I suppose we just have to look up *solicitors* in the yellow pages."

"You can't really go by the yellow pages, though, can you," Nick warned. "A chap at school who was trying to sell his motorbike said the dealers in the yellow pages were all crooks. He said word of mouth's better for most things."

"Motorbikes! Word of mouth? Do you think Mum wants to go round asking people how well they rate their divorce solicitors?" Liz asked, then, realising she had uttered the forbidden word for the first time, got up hastily and went to fetch the telephone directory.

Nick took it from her.

"I don't want one too near home," Flora told him. "But not too far away either, of course."

"There's Coffey, Sparrow and Samson in Bloxfield," he read out.

"Oh, I've seen them. They have that nice old Georgian building in the market square. Quite a large firm, I should think."

"Well, you'd want a large firm, Mum," Liz said. "I mean you'd need someone who specialises in –" she hesitated – "that sort of thing," she concluded lamely.

"So will you reply to this letter giving them the name and address of these Coffey people?"

"I imagine I must go to see them first, not that I've any experience. I'm not sure . . ." Her voice trailed off.

"That's what makes me so sick," Liz burst out. "He's been planning all this and you just get it thrown at you and you've no idea what to do or where to turn—"

"It's all right, Liz. I do know what I'm going to do. I'm going to ring these solicitors first thing on Monday morning and make an appointment to see them."

"Is that really what you want to do, Mum?"

"No, frankly I'd rather go to Marriage Guidance than a solicitor," Flora said.

"It's not called that any more, Mum. They're called Relate. Marriage Guidance went out with marriage."

Good old-fashioned marriage, whatever happened to it?

They all sat in silence for a while; it was so quiet in the kitchen that they could hear the ticking of the clock on the wall.

"I still think you ought to ring the grandparents," Liz said, breaking the silence at last. "I mean they're bound to be on your side. And if Dad really hasn't told them, I think we should get our word in first."

"I do hate to think of people having to take sides," her mother said, shaking her head. "Especially them."

"But you've always got on well with them and you and Ma are alike in a way."

"Nonsense, darling," Flora told her, laughing. "We're not a bit alike."

"Well, I mean you're alike in that you're both homely, the sort of people who bake cakes and are in when their children come in from school and all that."

Nick stopped buttering his croissant and said, "I've never thought that Mum and Ma were at all the same."

"I didn't say they were, stupid."

"Yes, you did, I heard you," Nick replied, returning to his croissant.

"I only said that they were alike in that neither of them had a career outside the home."

"Mum worked at home," Nick told her, his mouth full of croissant.

"But neither of them went out into the world."

"I don't see why she should. I bet there's as much world in here as there is out there."

"I'm not being critical, Nick. I'm just saying."

There was a ring at the back door.

"Oh, it's probably the man about the mower. Not the usual one. They're sending a chap called Woodcock," Nick explained, stuffing the last of the croissant into his mouth, getting up and going out.

"Put your anorak on," Flora called after him, "if you're going to be out in this lot."

Liz got up and stood by her mother's chair, putting her arms around her.

"It's all horrible," she said gently. "But you're going to have to go to the solicitor, aren't you?"

"I suppose so. I'd really rather have waited to hear from Duncan himself, but there it is."

"Would you like us to come with you?"

Flora shook her head.

"No, thanks, darling, but I'll consult you about anything and everything."

"We're still a family, Mum."

"Of course, of course. Oh, Liz, I am so sorry."

"Don't say that, Mum. You've nothing to apologise for."

The sound of the roar of an engine reached them from the yard.

"Sounds like Atco man is having some success," Liz said. "At least one thing's going right."

"It's a grand old mower, is this," Mr Woodcock told Nick. "They don't make 'em like this no more. Don't you never part with it."

He was a nutty little man, older than Nick had expected but a wizard with machinery. As he worked on the Atco he whistled between his two teeth, which seemed to be all he possessed. This, with his bright brown eyes and quizzical way of turning his head, gave him the look of an intelligent squirrel.

"Of course you have to nurse 'em along a bit," he conceded, as he removed the spark plug and set about cleaning it, "but they do a grand job, a grand job. The new tractors aren't a patch on them. Had one out for a customer yesterday and it wouldn't ride the bumps in the grass, not no way." He shook his head disapprovingly. "Just skimmed the top off down to bare earth. Did the same when you turned, however steady

90

you took it. Now this old friend'll ride the bumps like a beauty. No, don't you never part with this one. There now, let's give it a go, shall we," he suggested, patting the mower as if it were a horse, "give her a little run on the grass, see how she goes."

"Won't the grass be too wet?"

"No, the ground's dry underneath. There's been no rain for nigh on five weeks. And this is nobbut a drizzle. Where do you put the cut grass?"

"On the compost heap. I'll show you. But when Dad cuts the lawn he just empties the grass into a wheelbarrow and I run it down to the compost, if I'm about, that is. It saves him having to keep stopping."

"Your dad's not here today, then?"

Nick thought quickly.

"No, he wasn't able to be here," he said and felt quite pleased with his reply.

Mr Woodcock was looking around the shed.

"I see you've got a seat and roller for the machine over there."

"Yes, but Dad doesn't use them. He just walks behind."

"Why walk when you can sit?" Mr Woodcock asked, as he fitted the seat and roller on to the back of the mower. "And it does the lawn good to be rolled in the spring. Now on with the grass box and we're away."

He jumped on to the seat with the agility of a jockey jumping into the saddle and set off across the main lawn. Nick, following behind with a wheelbarrow, thought that the combination of contraption and driver looked like some hugely magnified insect.

Liz and her mother watched from the kitchen window, as Mr Woodcock whirred along and Nick followed. The grass was long and there was half an acre of it, so there was repeated stopping for the grass box to be emptied into the wheelbarrow, which Nick then trundled off to the compost heap. By the time he returned, the box was full again. Soon he was galloping, non-stop, between the Atco and the compost heap, his fair hair getting wilder all the time and his pink cheeks redder.

"He's got the worse job," Liz commented, laughing. "Jolly good exercise for him." Then, "What's wrong?" she asked suddenly.

"Nothing really. It's just that I've so often watched from this kitchen window while he did the grass collecting for his father. The two of them working together just like those two are doing now."

She shook her head, as if in disbelief.

"I know, Mum. I keep thinking that. I mean all these years, all the things we've done together, the holidays we've had, all that shared past, how could he throw it all away for someone he's known a couple of years?"

"I thought at the beginning," Flora said slowly, "that it was like a death, you know. But it's worse really because death destroys the present and the future, but he's somehow spoiled the past too. I wonder now if any of it was really worth anything to him?"

The rain had stopped and a watery sun was shining by the time they had finished mowing the lawn.

"Bring Mr Woodcock in for a drink," Flora told Nick when he came into the kitchen. "Where is he?"

"Unsaddling his horse in the shed, Mum. Probably rubbing it down and putting a blanket over it. He's great, I like him a lot. I'll go and bring him in."

So the four of them sat round the table eating fruit cake and drinking coffee.

"We must settle up with you, Mr Woodcock," Flora said.

"Nay. To tell you the truth when I heard about this trouble with an old Atco, I said I'd like to come. The youngsters were glad enough to be let off."

"But you cut the lawns as well."

"That was just to check the machine was running all right," he told her.

"All the same—"

"Any time you want a hand, let me know," he interrupted. "I'm retiring next month and I'll miss all my machines."

Like a groom missing his horses, Flora thought; that was a good comparison of Nick's.

"We might be very glad of your help," she said.

"There then, that's my number."

And he took a piece of paper out of one pocket and a stub of pencil from another and wrote down his telephone number.

"Tell your husband I'll come any time," he said, getting up and leaving them, after once again refusing payment.

Twelve

"I apologise for the long climb," Mr Coffey said, after his secretary had led her up three flights of stairs to his room at the very top of the old building. "I stay up here entirely for the view. It's very selfish of me."

It was a small room; a couple of steps took her across to the gabled windows, through which she saw the market square spread out far below, while at her eye level were the varied stone roofs of the old buildings across the way, all shapes and sizes of them, all higgledy-piggledy and at odd angles to each other, and above them all a long view of distant hills.

"I can understand your not wanting to leave it," she said, smiling as they shook hands.

He was a big man, round-faced, ruddy-cheeked, more like a farmer than a lawyer, she thought, not that she knew many lawyers, she mentally corrected herself, not yet anyway, pitched as she was so unexpectedly into their world.

The hand which took the letter from Duncan's solicitor was large, wide, square; a practical hand, she thought.

"What do you want to do, Mrs Maltby?" he asked when he had heard what she had to say and had read the letter.

"I don't want to rush anything. I mean I'd like to leave the door open for him to return."

"That's really what you and your children want?"

She tried to be honest.

"No, I don't think the children feel that at the moment. They're too hurt and angry. But in the long run, they'd be more secure if their father was at home. And," she added as an afterthought, "they wouldn't feel so responsible for me."

"Do they now?"

"Oh, yes. They never used to worry about us. There was no need. Their father and mother looked after each other and they were free to go off. But now they want to stay at home with me instead of getting on with their own lives."

"Isn't that a good thing? That children should care for their parents?"

"No, not at this stage. I mean if I was very old and they were middle-aged, of course they should look after an elderly parent, but they're at the age when they should be flying the nest and I'm of an age when I should be able to manage without them."

"And if he doesn't come back?"

"Then I just want to start remaking my life on my own, so that the children and I can be as independent as possible."

"I have to say to you, Mrs Maltby, that if you want to be independent and make a new life for yourself, your best course is to go for a quick divorce."

"Oh, no, that really isn't what I want."

"Well, shall we just see what his solicitors come up with? There's very little we can do until we know that."

He handed her back the letter.

"You reply giving them my name and address and when I hear from them and what they propose on your husband's behalf, I'll let you know, so that we can meet again and discuss their proposals."

So it was all over very quickly; they said farewell, her hand momentarily disappearing into his great paw, and she made her way down three flights of stairs and out into the square.

She had planned to do some shopping in Bloxfield but instead made straight for the car, suddenly afraid of meeting people, of being asked questions, of having to make conversation. She just wanted to be back in the safety of her own home, like an animal retreating into its lair.

95

There were two ways of getting back. She'd come by the quick route on the dual carriageway, just wanting to get to Bloxfield, find a place to park, not be late for her appointment. But she'd go back by the country road, a road which wound its way through villages and hamlets, past wayside pubs and steepled churches. She hadn't been this way for a while, she thought as she approached the long avenue of trees which almost met overhead, so that even on the hottest summer days the road was cool and shadowy. There were bluebell woods behind the trees, an azure haze glimpsed like a distant lake through the foliage.

She used to bring the children here when they were little and they would pick the flowers which were always sticky and drooping by the time they got home; wild flowers aren't designed for vases, she'd tell them as they stuffed their bedraggled booty into water, and it's probably illegal to pick them anyway. How long ago it now seemed, a different life.

It was nearly three weeks now, three weeks since he had gone, she reflected as she drove down this shady road, and still she seemed to be living in limbo. Nothing had been clarified in that time and it looked as if it could drag on like this for months. She had some money in the building society; that would last for a little while anyway. This morning she'd had something from the gas company about an unpaid bill, which was nonsense as they were all paid by direct debit.

Suddenly she realised: he'd closed the joint account and he'd cancelled all those standing orders, that's what he'd done. The rest would be writing soon: the water, the electricity, council tax, telephone, all of them. If only she'd thought of this sooner, she could have asked the solicitor what to do. How in the world were they going to live?

She was on the wrong road; she didn't recognise where she was. She hadn't been this way before. She must have missed the turning to the left after the long winding road emerged from the trees. She must have gone straight over the cross-roads. She was hopeless; she couldn't even find her way home along a road she'd known for years. She felt herself begin to shake, she felt sweat break out on her forehead. She pulled into the side of the road and turned off the engine. She sat in the car, trembling and breathless.

So this is what a panic attack means, is it? Keep calm, Flora, she told herself. You have plenty of petrol, you can read a map and anyway all you need to do is turn round and go back to the crossroads. There is no need to panic. But part of her knew that this attack had nothing to do with losing her way and everything to do with the shock of Duncan's disappearance. Must keep calm about that too, she told herself, addressing herself as if she was a separate person, trust Mr Coffey to sort it out, that's what he's there for. It's his job. He deals with this kind of thing every day of his life, not like me who's never dealt with anything like it before, and never for a moment thought I'd have to.

Gradually the shaking stopped, the panic retreated though she was aware that it was still there, threateningly near, like some prowling animal beating a temporary retreat. She was very weary, her confidence badly shaken, but calmer now, she started up the car and drove slowly back home.

"What did he say, Mum? What's he like?" Nick asked as soon as she got back.

"Sh, Nick, let her get indoors," Liz told him, taking her mother's coat and then leading her into the kitchen. "Look it's all ready and the kettle's boiling. I thought you'd be hungry because you hardly had any lunch. I've made us a sort of high tea, like Gran has. It's a bit high on carbohydrates, I'm afraid."

"Oh, thank you, darling. It looks lovely. I'll just pop up and see her."

"No, she's all right," Liz said, pressing on her mother's shoulders to keep her sitting down. "She's fed and watered and playing patience."

Flora was well aware that Liz was just as eager as Nick to hear what she had to report. They'd both been building high hopes on this meeting, she could see it in their eyes. People pin expectations on a meeting with a solicitor, like they do on hospital tests.

"I'm sorry," she said. "There's really no news."

Their faces fell.

"He must have said something," Nick objected.

"Just that he's taken us on and I'll see him again when he's heard from your father's solicitors."

Odd how she kept referring to him as their father nowadays rather than as Duncan, her husband. She never used to do that. Presumably it was because she'd found out that although he'd always be their father, being her husband had proved to be a less permanent relationship.

"He didn't give you any advice at all?"

"He asked me what I wanted to do and I said not to rush into anything. Ideally we'd just like him to come back."

Nick and Liz looked at each other but said nothing.

"Then he did say that if we wanted to be independent we should go for a quick divorce."

"We think, Nick and I," Liz said, taking a deep breath, "that if he doesn't want us, we don't want him. We can do without him."

"But we can't do without his money," Nick pointed out. "Well, some of it, anyway."

"We've been talking while you've been out," Liz began.

"I thought so," Flora said, smiling. "I smelled a plot."

They all laughed. When they were little and planning surprises, as children do, they used to ask her afterwards if she'd smelled a plot. She'd always denied it, of course.

"I'm going to go on working at shelf-filling or anything else I can get—"

"No, Nick, you must go off as you'd planned."

"Later maybe, there's all the summer, but I want to earn as much as I can ready for college. We don't know if Dad's going to cough up now, or how much. And —" he shrugged — "I just want to be around a bit."

"Me too," Liz said.

"But you're going off to France next month."

"No, I've scrubbed that. Maybe later, but I thought I'd get a part-time job here near home—"

"But you need the language practice."

"Look, Mum, I have an extra year later on to work in France and Germany. And I'm pretty fluent."

"What sort of job?"

"I thought I might be useful in schools in the summer term. Or I did think of advertising for a coaching job, but part-time so I can be at home quite a bit. If I'm at home you won't have to worry about Gran and you'll be free to go and see solicitors or apply for jobs—"

"I thought you were against that idea?"

"We were only against your pushing yourself too soon. We've talked it over and we quite see that, even apart from the money, you'll need something when we're away after next autumn and Dad's not here."

"And Gran?"

Again they exchanged glances.

"We think she should go permanently into the home."

"Not yet. And it's too expensive."

"Exactly. We think you should tell her finance man that he should fork out to pay her bills there."

"But it isn't just the money, Liz. She's really not bad enough yet to go there permanently. She's much more compos mentis than most of the others. And she's quite happy here."

"You could have fooled me."

"I know she's sometimes difficult—"

"Bloody ungrateful would be nearer the mark."

"But she's pretty settled," Flora went on, ignoring the interruption.

"Anyway, that's what Liz and I think, Mum," Nick said, looking at his watch. "I'll have to go soon."

"Take the car, Nick. I really don't like your cycling so much at night-time. That road to the supermarket is unlit and very winding."

"Thanks. I have to admit that my back light failed last night."

"Nick! *Never* cycle without lights at night. You're absolutely invisible to cars. You should know how dangerous it is now you're a driver yourself."

"OK, Mum."

"Promise me. Swear."

"I-swear-by-almighty-God-and-cross-my-heart-swelp-me-God."

Flora refused to smile.

"Why do you have to do the night shift anyway?" she asked instead.

"Partly because it's better paid, but mostly because it gives me more time here during the day and Liz and I have a plan."

"Yes, we've had an idea, Mum, about something we can do here."

"What's that?"

"Redecorate the house."

"*What?*"

"Yes, make it feel like a new start."

Oh, God, where did they get all the energy from? They were blithely proposing to take on jobs, help her with the garden and Gran, and now redecorate the house. Had they any idea what it would involve? She stared at them, at these young, eager faces, full of plans and confidence. Who was she, old, rejected, disillusioned and weary, to dissuade them?

She looked from one to the other.

"I think you're marvellous," she said.

"Bloody marvellous," Liz agreed.

Thirteen

Flora lay awake that night, reliving the events of the day, hearing again what Liz and Nick had said. The more she thought about it, the more the thought of the pair of them chucking paint around the house filled her with horror. And horror is never more horrible than at two o'clock in the morning. Better to do something practical about it, she thought as she got up and went to look in the cupboard on the landing. Plenty of dustsheets there. And some old heavy linen sheets banished from beds long ago when terylene ones came in. Enough to protect all the carpets in the house.

It was a cold night; she shivered when she got back into bed, got up again and went to fill a hot water bottle.

They'd been so good, Liz and Nick, she told herself; she should be glad of that rather than fret about carpets. After Nick had gone to work this evening she'd had a long talk with Liz, explaining that she wanted to invite Duncan back to discuss things. If they could all just sit round the kitchen table and talk, not necessarily about money, just family arrangements, surely they could sort something out? They'd always done that for lesser things, why not now? She was convinced that if he could just come back and be made to feel part of his family again, be welcomed home, he would see reason. And if he didn't, well at least they'd given it a try and nothing was lost.

Liz hadn't thought it a good idea, in fact had thought it could make things worse, but she'd listened and then helped her compose a letter to Duncan, marking it personal and addressing it care of his solicitors with a request that it should be forwarded. Yes, together they'd done it and together they'd posted it in the letter box on the corner of the road.

What was Duncan doing now, she wondered as she lay in bed clutching the bottle. In bed with Fiona from Publicity, of course. She must try not to think about it. But oh, how could he, she found herself demanding, how could he just walk out and not give a thought for them and how they were going to manage? After all these years of planning things together, always putting the family first? Hadn't it entered his head that Nick and Liz would give up their plans, stay at home? What right had he to turn the lives of his own children upside down, just to satisfy some whim of his own?

Liz shouldn't make this sacrifice; she *ought* to go to France, even though she was much more fluent than her mother now. She smiled as she remembered the first time they had taken Liz, ten years old and top in French, to France. They had stayed in a *gîte* in Brittany, a cottage in the grounds of a country house belonging to an old lady, Madame Gagneux, who let it to eke out her war widow's pension.

She was a delightful old lady, who spoke perfect English. "Please don't talk to my daughter in English," Flora had begged. "We do want her to speak French." This the young Liz had steadfastly refused to do. She would listen to her mother, afterwards remarking, "You should have used the subjunctive after, '*Il faut que*', Mum" or "The future perfect of *aller* is *je serai allée*." Oh yes, she'd understood all right, but utter a word of French herself she would not. Sent to buy bread and milk at the local shop she would acquire it by the simple expedient of helping herself to what she needed and handing over the money, without a word spoken.

It was infuriating, especially as they'd planned the holiday partly to help her improve her spoken French. Mothers have murdered for less, Flora told her years later. One morning, however, fate seemed to play into her hands. Liz broke an eggcup. "You must go to Madame," Flora had told her, seizing the opportunity, "And apologise. Say we'll replace it if she'll tell you where she bought it." Pleased with this ploy, she had watched as Liz trotted off down the path to Madame's house. She returned smiling cheerfully.

"She says it's all right, it's only cheap, but if you're worried you can get one at the little general store in the square or on the china stall in Wednesday's market."

Flora had been so pleased to think that Liz had at last opened up and had this quite complicated conversation that she'd hugged her daughter as she said, "Well done darling, so you had a good talk in French?"

"No."

"Oh. So Madame talked to you in English?"

"No."

"Liz, how did you manage all this talk about eggcups?"

"Sign language."

She smiled now as she remembered. How golden all those holidays seemed in retrospect. Not only that one in Brittany, but the one the following year in Normandy in a farm cottage that was perfect except that it was downwind of the piggeries. And the one on the edge of the forest when the weather had been so cold when they arrived that the children had demanded to go home, but then a courteous old lady, the farmer's mother, had brought over a huge double saw and handed it to Duncan, waved invitingly in the direction of the local forest and said, *"Servez-vous, Monsieur."* And they had indeed helped themselves to the forest, Nick and Duncan going foraging there, dragging back great branches which they sawed up and fed into the huge fireplace which filled one wall of the cottage and was fringed with an elaborately embroidered cloth hanging from the mantelshelf. By that great fire they had played all the usual games; rummy, snap and even, God help us, Happy Families!

She remembered the time in another part of Brittany when the owners of the cottage were away and all their needs were supplied by a Monsieur Vigaroux who saw to the rubbish,

103

mended the washing machine and left a pile of home-grown vegetables on their doorstep every morning. When he asked if there was anything the children missed, she had laughed and said, "Only their guinea pigs," which had been left at home in the care of friends. She should have known. "I have guinea-pigs," he'd said. "I have forty-eight guinea pigs. The children can come and see them any time."

Liz and Nick had been delighted.

"How kind of him to keep so many," they kept exclaiming. "And rabbits too. Most grown-ups wouldn't bother."

She'd managed to keep from them the purpose of Mr Vigaroux's menagerie; fortunately Liz's French wasn't up to understanding the significance of Monsieur Vigaroux's saying, "Just a sharp tap on the nose and plenty of garlic."

Their last family holiday was in a longboat on the canal when Liz and Nick got so good at leaping out to work the locks that she and Duncan just stayed on board and left them to it, realising that now they really were capable of managing unsupervised.

"We'll be surplus to requirements soon," they had agreed.

Had he really believed that? Such a silly thing to say, even in jest. Her pillow was wet with tears. She hadn't realised that she must have been crying all the time she'd thought she was enjoying these memories. Even the past is spoiled, she thought again.

She heard a little sound, a little clicking sound as Liz's bedroom door opened. On her way to the loo probably. So she couldn't sleep either. Maybe she'd like a hot drink.

She got up and went on to the landing. Liz was half way down the stairs, going slowly, holding the bannister. She knew that deliberate way of walking. When she was little Liz had walked in her sleep.

Very quietly she followed her, careful not to make a sound that might wake her. Liz walked confidently across the hall and made for the back door.

"Come back to bed, Liz," Flora said gently.

"The back door's locked."

"Yes. That's all right."

"Don't lock him out. He's in the garden. Dad's in the garden."

She didn't know what to say.

"Let him in," the sleeping Liz went on. "He might want to come in from the garden."

"He's got a key if he wants to come in."

"Oh, then that's all right," Liz said, smiling in her sleep as she let her mother lead her back upstairs.

It was a happier, more carefree smile than she ever had in the daytime nowadays. She was still smiling as Flora tucked her into bed and left her to sleep.

She herself slept no more that night. Nor did she lie thinking of the past, only worrying about the future.

Fourteen

I t was quiet in the superstore at six o'clock in the morning. The late night shoppers had gone home to bed and the early morning shoppers usually didn't arrive until seven. The place had a ghostly feel, Nick thought as he pushed his trolley down deserted aisles to the Home Baking area and began to unload.

He didn't mind the job; he quite liked heaving heavy weights about and arranging packets and tins in neat rows on shelves. It was his fellow shelf-fillers he didn't care for, especially his contemporaries. They ganged up, these young men did, and were particularly horrible to Lenny, the only old one among them, mocking him, telling him he was past it because he couldn't heave boxes around as easily as they could, drawing conclusions about his sex life. He couldn't understand why they picked on Lenny for their bullying, because he was easily the nicest of the bunch. Lenny it was who had helped him when he arrived, shown him where to go and what to do, filling out the manager's hasty and inadequate instructions. Lenny was the only one who'd bothered with him at all and who, even now, kept an eye on him to make sure he did things right. He didn't say any of this at home; he'd made up his mind he was going to stick it out until term started.

He was arranging packets of cornflour on a top shelf when a woman said, "Excuse me, could you tell me where I'll find packets of dates?"

He turned round, desperately trying to think where dates might be found. They were supposed to know the whereabouts of everything. It was all right for customers not to be able to find what they wanted, the manager had told him, because the more they wandered about looking for things, the more they bought, but it was very bad for the firm's reputation if it was perceived that the staff didn't know where things were either.

So, "Dates?" he repeated to himself. Ah yes, boxes of dates, he'd seen boxes of dates at the end of aisle nineteen.

"I don't mean in boxes, I mean in blocks," the woman said.

"Packets of dates will be among the sultanas and currants," he said, pleased with himself for remembering.

"No. I don't want the ready chopped sort rolled in sugar. I want blocks of dates. I'm afraid I know exactly what I want."

She smiled as she spoke. She was good-looking in a hard sort of way. Yes, she looked as if she knew exactly what she wanted and would get it.

"It's to make some sort of sticky confection my partner likes," she said. "I suspect his wife used to make it," she added with a funny, conspiratorial little smile.

Now he knew what she wanted; his mother made something with blocks of dates; he'd seen her chopping them up on the back of the bread board. He spotted a block of something on the shelf and handed it to her.

"No, that's marzipan," she told him, handing back the offering.

They both searched, he looking on the higher shelves, she on the lower.

"Found them," she said. "No wonder we missed them, right down there," and she put two packets into her trolley and went off down the aisle, collecting tins and packets on the way, while he returned to arranging his cartons of cornflour.

"I must say it was a good idea of yours to get the shopping done on the way back from the airport, darling," a man's voice called to her.

"Well, it's nice to get it over with, so we can go straight to bed when we get home."

"That sounds a *very* good idea," the man replied, intoning

the words in such a way as to make the sexual implication quite clear.

Nick turned round, recognising his father's voice.

Duncan was only a few feet away. He looked directly at his son, averted his eyes and began to walk past.

Nick never understood what happened next. Of its own volition his right hand made itself into a fist and he, who had never hit anyone in his life, slammed it into his father's face with an upper cut which a professional boxer might have envied.

Duncan fell over backwards against the shelves. Little tins of baking powder cascaded to the ground, barrels of custard rolled down the aisle and a bag of sugar exploded, spewing out its contents on to the polished floor.

Nick didn't give it or his father a second glance; he walked away and didn't stop until he got out into the loading bay. There he paused, his heart pounding, and waited for the world's wrath to descend on him. He didn't know what form it would take: shrieking Fionas, bruised fathers, furious managers waving dismissal notices in his face, any or all of this would happen.

But nothing did. He stood there and everything was quiet. At the far end some of the men were already leaving, one or two loading up. After what seemed like hours but was probably only a few minutes, he felt, like a criminal forced to revisit the scene of his crime, impelled to go back to the Home Baking aisle. Tins and cartons were still strewn about, but there was no sign of Duncan or Fiona from Publicity. Quickly he picked up the merchandise, putting anything that looked a bit battered at the back of the shelves, and went to fetch a brush to sweep up the sugar.

Lenny was emerging from the broom cupboard, holding a brush and dustpan.

"I was just on my way," he said. "Thought you might need a hand."

Together they went back and swept up the sugar. There was

still nobody about in the aisle, nobody except Lenny seemed to be aware that anything unusual had happened. And how much Lenny had seen, Nick couldn't know and didn't ask. The older man made no comment except to say, "Least said, soonest mended," as they returned the brush to the cupboard.

Incredible though it seemed, Nick thought as he drove home, it was just possible that nobody need ever know what had happened. His father would probably never tell anyone, he himself wouldn't mention it to a soul, not even Liz. He wondered what that woman made of it, not that it mattered, he told himself as he put the car into the garage and went into the kitchen.

Liz was up already.

"Mum's with Gran," she said. "Golly, you look shattered. Busy night?"

He nodded.

"Shall I make you some scrambled eggs while you eat your cornflakes?"

"Thanks, that would be great."

She came over and sat next to him while he ate.

"Mum wrote to Dad last night," she told him, pouring them each a mug of coffee, "suggesting that he might come and see us for what she called a calm and reasonable talk—"

He dropped his spoon into his cornflakes, splashing milk.

"But he won't come now!" he exclaimed. "Oh, my God, I've torn it."

"What do you mean?"

"Oh, well, nothing."

"Come on, Nick—"

"No, really, it's nothing. I wasn't thinking."

"Oh yes, you were. What have you been up to? I won't tell Mum."

"Well, it's Dad."

"Yes?"

"He came into the store—"

"Last night?"

"Well, this morning. With her."

"Good God, what did you do?"

"I hit him."

"Where?"

"In the Home Bakery aisle."

"Oh, Nick, I didn't mean that. I meant which bit of him did you hit?"

"My fist seemed to go for his head. His face I suppose, sort of. I didn't plan it, Liz, honestly."

She was staring at him, shaking her head in disbelief. Nick of all people.

"Well, you're right, Nick," she said at last. "He certainly won't come now for that reasonable discussion."

"He might be a bit bruised. My hand's quite sore."

Suddenly she began to laugh. He looked at her, surprised.

"I thought you'd be cross," he said.

"No, I'm proud of you. I'm sorry your hand's sore, but it was hurt in a good cause."

"You think so? Even though I've wrecked this meeting Mum wants?"

"Well, I wasn't too hopeful about that anyway. I reckon it would have been a fearful strain, everybody being polite and nobody knowing what to say, Mum wanting it to be all sensible and friendly, Dad being uncooperative because basically he feels guilty—"

"He didn't sound as if he felt guilty last night. You should have heard the way he spoke to her – Yuk!"

"That was why you hit him, was it?"

Nick shrugged.

"Maybe partly," he admitted, "maybe because of the way he cut me, walked past, just the way he's walked out on us. I don't know, honestly, Liz."

"Nick," Liz began, not liking to ask, but nonetheless wanting to know, "What did she look like?"

"I didn't notice," Nick said, unwilling to admit that he'd thought she was quite pretty, when he didn't know who she was.

"Oh, well, let's not worry about them. It's what your employers will do that matters more. Somebody is bound to have seen."

Nick shook his head.

"You've no idea how quiet it can be sometimes at night. Really not a customer in sight and not many staff around anyway. They're thinking of giving up one of the all-night openings. It was just like a ghost town this morning from about five o'clock onwards."

"But if anyone did see, you could be in trouble. There must be something in your contract about how you behave—"

"Oh, yes, we're supposed to be polite to the customers at all times. We're not supposed to hit them."

She laughed and got up.

"In a court of law maybe we could plead that it wasn't a customer but a father that you hit. Look, I'm a barrister," she went on, putting a tea towel over her head as a wig, "This man was *in loco parentis*, not *loco emptoris*, M'Lud," she pronounced in solemn, legal tones. "And as such we deem him worthy to be socked in the jaw. And now," whippping off the tea towel, "I'm going to make you those well-deserved scrambled eggs and get you off to bed before Mum comes down."

He yawned and stretched.

"Thanks, Liz," he said, watching her as she broke eggs into a bowl and began beating them with a fork.

"For what?"

"For not minding that I've made a mess of that meeting Mum wanted."

"I've told you. I don't think it would have worked anyway. I think we're better off with honest-to-goodness old-fashioned open warfare. I don't want Mum to crawl, I want her to fight. And," she told him as she tipped the frothy yellow mixture into a saucepan, "You've given just the right signal for that."

"What's all this about signals?" Flora asked, coming into the kitchen.

111

"We're just agreeing we should all present a united front," Liz said calmly, tipping scrambled eggs on to toast and taking the plate over to Nick.

"You two always did that, when you were in trouble," Flora said, sitting down at the table. "Yes, thanks, Liz," she added as Liz waved the coffee at her. "I'd love a cup."

As she drank it she looked at her daughter and tried to identify this capable young woman with the girl who had walked in her sleep last night, who had seemed so fragile and hurt. We're all three of us like that in a way, she thought, sometimes utterly downcast, sometimes angry, sometimes determined and brave, never quite sure which way we'll be when we wake up in the morning. But it's worse for them; they're new arrivals in the adult world, still young enough to feel homesick sometimes for the secure and happy land of childhood. The world in which I brought them up, she thought sadly, did not prepare them for this.

Fifteen

"If only I'd known that Duncan was going to do this," Flora confided to her daughter one afternoon, "I might have taken that offer of a job from Edgar Monroe more seriously."

"You once told me never to say *if only*," Liz reminded her.

"Did I?" She smiled and reached out to touch her hand. "Then you must do as I say, and not as I do," she told her.

They both laughed, then, "Why don't you ring him and ask if the job's still going?" Liz asked.

"Oh, I couldn't. It was a while ago and he was really keen to get on with things. He's an impatient person, he'll have fixed everything up by now."

"Well, I think you should try, just the same."

When her mother shook her head, she went on more brusquely, "The right job isn't going to fall into your lap, you know, Mum. You'll have to make an effort to get it. That is, of course, if you really do want a job."

"And then there's always the problem of your grandmother."

"Well, you know what Nick and I think about that," Liz told her. "Go on, show a bit of fight, be a devil, ring the man. Like *now*, Mum."

So it had really been to please her daughter, or at least to show that she did have some spirit left in her, that she'd made that telephone call, sure herself that it would be fruitless.

But Edgar Monroe was delighted to hear from her.

"I did think of ringing you," he said, "but you were so sure about turning me down last time."

"So you haven't found anyone else?"

"Oh, I did. An admirably qualified young man but he's gone off on some research grant to Australia. I'm seeing people this week. When can you come and see me? How about Friday?"

On Friday morning she was seeing her solicitor.

"I have an appointment in Bloxfield at half-past nine," she said. "I could catch a train from there to Victoria at about eleven, I should think, and be with you by midday."

Liz was triumphant.

"I told you, didn't I?" she exclaimed, hugging her mother.

"Yes, you were right, but I have to find out more about it, this is really only an interview, darling. Don't be too hopeful. And then if I am offered the job there's still the problem of your grandmother."

"Oh, it'll work out somehow," Liz reassured her airily. "But why don't you drive up? You always used to. What's the point of leaving the car in Bloxfield?"

Flora hesitated, not wanting to admit that she was nervous of driving in London now that her confidence had been so shattered and anyway hadn't felt the same about driving since that ridiculous panic attack.

"Oh, it's just that the parking's so awful in London," she said instead.

The only response to her invitation to Duncan to come to talk things over with them, had been an impersonal message from his solicitor saying that his client did not think such a meeting would be productive. It had been worth a try, Flora consoled herself as she drove along the dual carriageway to Bloxfield, trying not to be too much hurt by this latest rejection.

It seemed longer than a month since her last visit to Mr Coffey for their lives had in the meantime taken on such a different pattern: Nick, who should have been backpacking in India, was working every night at the superstore, coming home at six in the morning and sleeping until lunchtime. Liz, who should have been studying in France, was travelling each day to nearby Foxted, coaching a little girl whose illness was keeping her off school for the summer term. Liz went every morning to teach her languages and English while a young unemployed graduate coped with maths and science in the afternoons. "Her mother thinks she can dispense with history and geography for a term," Liz said cheerfully. She had only walked in her sleep once more and that was within two days of her first nocturnal prowling; since then she seemed to have settled.

They were starting to decorate her bedroom today, the pair of them. Once upon a time, in that old life, she wouldn't have dreamed of letting them loose in there with cans of paint, but now it seemed more important not to dampen their enthusiasm than it was to protect her carpets. So maybe all of them were changing their values.

"I know the way," she told the secretary who offered to guide her along the corridor and up the stairs to Mr Coffey's room. Already she felt she belonged here, didn't feel ill at ease just by being in a solicitor's office. Nor was she uneasy now with the bulky Mr Coffey in his little room overlooking the square.

"Well, now," he said, after she had sat down, "they're offering a clean break settlement."

A clean break! What an extraordinary phrase to describe ending the messy, everyday business of marriage with all its interrupted, unfinished routines. More suitable to the pruning of roses. Good sharp secateurs leave no broken stems, no snagged branches.

"They point out that the advantage of a clean break settlement is that it puts the control of the money entirely into your hands and avoids the constant renegotiating, arguing about his resources and your resources, changes in circumstances and so on."

115

"Oh, yes. We want to avoid that for everyone's sake."

"They're offering that you should keep the house and accept a lump sum of twenty-five thousand pounds."

She was surprised. It seemed a great deal of money for Duncan to part with so suddenly.

"Which you would invest, of course, to provide an income."

He picked up a letter from his desk, the one that she had written to him last week.

"I have your letter here about the non-payment of household bills and have spoken to your husband's solicitors about that. It has been agreed that he will pay your legal expenses and be responsible for household bills until a settlement is finalised."

"Oh, thank goodness."

It's true, she thought, the old cliché about relief flooding through you. She could feel it, physically feel it, flowing through her veins.

"I couldn't really believe he'd just not pay our bills."

But she had believed it; in the wee small hours of the night she had imagined the electricity being turned off, then the gas and the water.

Mr Coffey's smile was cynical.

"I expect his solicitor made it clear to him that he couldn't get away with it," he said. "Furthermore, if he wants a quick divorce, he'll behave himself," he added with unexpected severity. She had a champion in Mr Coffey, she realised and found the thought comforting.

"So what happens next?"

"I think you must go away and consider the offer," he told her. "See what income you could derive from the suggested sum and then decide if such an income is adequate. In the meantime I will write to your husband's solicitors asking for voluntary disclosure of his financial situation. When I receive a reply, we can talk again about whether the offer is a fair one."

"Will there be much delay then?"

He shook his head.

"No, I don't think so. And it helps that his solicitor is a member of the Family Law Association, as I am. We always try to settle if at all possible."

Of course, they probably know each other, she realised, as she walked downstairs. On the half-landing she paused and looked down at the square, which was busy with people shopping, going in and out of offices, greeting each other. They probably inhabit this same town, Duncan's solicitor and mine, she thought. Perhaps they meet for lunch, over there at The Crown, as Duncan and I sometimes used to meet long ago, in that other life.

She left the car at the station and took the train to Victoria. It crawled along, an adenoidal guard explaining that this was due to engine trouble, but in the end she was only fifteen minutes late for her twelve o'clock appointment with Edgar Monroe.

"I'm delighted you're interested in the project after all," he said, shaking her hand. "Truly delighted."

His craggy old face really did seem to light up with pleasure. Not that he was really old, it was just that his face seemed to have been around for a long time and taken more than its fair share of battering. The skin was furrowed and loose as if it had been made big enough for him to grow into and, when he had failed to do so, had fallen into folds. He had a lolloping kind of walk, his long arms swinging and his legs somehow not quite in rhythm with the rest of his body. He always reminded Flora of those lines, "A yellow-eyed collie was guarding his coat, loose-limbed and loblolly, though wise and remote." Edgar wasn't remote and she wasn't sure if he was wise, but loose-limbed and loblolly he certainly was.

His Scottish accent was slight, but revealed itself in the clarity of his consonants, the roll of his R's, the richness of the way he pronounced a *"wh"* sound. She noticed voices and found his attractive.

"It will mean we shall see more of you," he was saying, "and that's very nice, but I'm also pleased because I'm quite sure you're the right person for the job."

"Tell me more about it."

"Right, but you'll have some coffee?"

"I'd love that."

He telephoned briefly and then went on, "It's a new departure for us. There is a need, we think, for the sort of biography sixth formers can benefit from and enjoy. There should be something to bridge the gap between the history book they use for GCSE and the standard biographies they'll be expected to read at college."

"You mean something between the chapter on Gladstone in the school text book and Morley's *Life of Gladstone* in three volumes?"

"Exactly. We need to lead them more gently from the text book to works of real scholarship. We aim to produce biographies of the leading nineteenth-century Prime Ministers, which are readable but thoroughly researched and of the highest standard. We must avoid the drily academic, but we must also avoid oversimplification. The young can perfectly well cope with complex ideas if they're properly presented."

She nodded.

"Now we are trying to get together a team of historians, preferably with some teaching experience. I think you would be an ideal person, Flora. You have a particular love of the nineteenth century, your style is clear and direct and you would inject humour and, above all, readability. And you have the scholarship to do it."

"Thank you."

"Of course, we're still in the early stages. We plan to get our team together to discuss how it shall be done when the academic year starts in the autumn. It would mean you'd have to travel up here three times a week at first. After that obviously your work would be mainly in the libraries. What do you think? Ah, thank you, Janet," he added as the coffee arrived.

Flora hesitated, glad of a moment to think while she took the coffee, added milk, stirred it.

"It will depend on getting help with my mother. She lives with me and is getting, well, a little confused. But in principle, yes, I'd love to come."

He went on to discuss details, down to which office she would have, which secretary she would share. His enthusiasm was infectious. She was carried along by it.

"I really will let you know for certain when I've settled things on the domestic front," she said, preparing to leave. "But apart from that, I have no problem about accepting the job."

"Something puzzles me," he said, in his forthright way. "When I first asked you two or three months ago, you were definitely not interested. Indeed you hardly considered it. That was when I advertised and got the young man who has just let us down. What made you change your mind?"

She hesitated. She had quite decided that her private life would not encroach on the world of work. They were to be kept apart.

"Of course, it's none of my business," Edgar said. "I stand reproved."

"Oh, no please, it's not that."

She couldn't bear him to feel rebuked. That had not been what she intended, especially after he'd been so kind.

"It's just that things have changed at home," she explained. "Since I spoke to you that first time, Duncan, my husband, has left me."

The awful, hackneyed phrase hung in the air. She stared at him, embarrassed for having spoken. She wished her words unsaid.

To her surprise, he got up, put an arm around her shoulders and said, "Come along out for lunch."

She was taken aback; he'd never done such a thing before, indeed had a reputation for meanness.

"Thank you," she said. "I'd like that, very much."

It wasn't a particularly grand or fashionable restaurant, but very comfortable and relaxed. He found a table for them in a quiet corner.

"We'll order the wine now," he said, "and have a glass while we look at the menu. Have you any preferences?"

"No, I'm sure you know more about wine than I do. I'll leave you to choose; I'm off to the Ladies."

In the cloakroom, she realised how glad she was that she'd dressed up for what she'd thought of as an interview, but which was proving to be more of an occasion. She'd lost weight, she observed in the long glass, and that was no bad thing. Her light summer suit didn't stretch across her stomach any more, nor tend to go in under her buttocks. There were flatnesses where once there had been incipient bulges. For the first time in weeks, it mattered to her what she looked like. She combed her hair, improved her make-up, gave herself an approving look in the glass and went back to her host.

"The home-made soup's really excellent here," he said. "Good old vegetable broth like my mother used to make. Except of course that she'd never have served it with garlic bread, bless her. She'd have thought that was dreadfully foreign."

"Do you go back to Scotland still?"

He shook his head.

"I've no family left up there now. My wife used to like to go back to see friends, but since I lost her, I've had no cause to return."

By *lost her*, what did he mean? Once she would have assumed death, but now she was less sure.

Scotch salmon and new potatoes followed the broth as they talked of work and of his plans for the new department. They talked of families too and very briefly she described to him what had happened, omitting details like those dreadful notes Duncan had left them – not that they were details in her mind, the shock of them would live in her for ever, but they were omissible in this context. She told him the good things, the positive things like Nick and Liz getting jobs, like finding splendid Mr Woodcock who understood the vagaries of the Atco. She didn't mention the decorating, trying not to think of paint-splashed carpets.

Afterwards she took a taxi back to Victoria; it was an extravagance which fitted her newly relaxed mood, due to the wine and good food and being treated like a woman, being spoiled. It had been a successful day. For the first time she felt confident that it would all work out in the end, now that Mr Coffey was sorting out her affairs and that she was going to get a properly paid job. Somehow or other she would find a carer for her mother. There must be some kindly soul who would like a job that didn't really need any training, just patience and a certain childishness perhaps.

It was gloomy and overcast by the time the train drew into Bloxfield station; she felt suddenly very tired as she made her way to the car park. She tried to recapture the optimism of the afternoon, the euphoria of the taxi ride, but it had all evaporated with the wine. She took the dual carriageway home.

The house seemed very quiet. Nobody answered when she called out to them in the kitchen. As she went upstairs she could hear voices in her bedroom.

"Careful," Nick shouted, as she tried to open the door. "There's a ladder in the way."

The room was emptied of furniture except for the bed and wardrobe which they'd pushed to the centre. They'd stripped the paper off the walls and were painting the ceiling. She could see that they were making a thoroughly professional job of it. The dustsheets covered everything, not a bit of carpet was visible. The wallpaper had been stowed neatly away in three large black plastic bin bags. Nick was wearing his father's overalls, Liz an old cotton dress and a bath cap.

In the centre of the room sat her mother, wrapped in a dustsheet and evidently very happy.

"We brought her down, Mum," Liz explained. "She was getting a bit bored up there on her own and we wanted to get on, so it seemed best to have her in with us. She's been fine."

"The walls are all peeling," her mother said. "They must have caught the sun."

Sixteen

"You've lost weight," Milly said. "I hope you're not neglecting yourself?"

"No, I'm fine."

"Well, I'm glad to hear it."

The big brown eyes were moist with sympathy and understanding.

"I really just called in to check that you were all right. If I can help in any way, you only have to ask, you know."

"You'll come in for a cup of tea?" Flora invited, thinking she couldn't really in all decency keep the woman on the doorstep any longer.

"Well, just a quickie. Can I bring Sammy out of the car for a run in your nice garden?"

"Sammy?" Flora asked, for some reason thinking of toddlers.

"He's my friend's spaniel. They're away for two months and I've said I'll look after him. Blessedly he's house-trained."

Sammy may have been house-trained, but he certainly wasn't garden-trained, Flora observed as he scampered over flower beds and vegetable plots, cocked his leg against every tree and finally emptied his bowels in the middle of the lawn.

"We'll have tea in the kitchen. It's a bit cold outside," she said. "And the children are decorating the drawing room."

"You've got them decorating for you? Well, I suppose everyone must muck in when times are hard. You've been busy, I see," she observed, looking at the kitchen table.

It was covered in papers. Flora had spent the past days

exploring every avenue to find out the best income she could get from her twenty-five thousand pounds. For one who had never taken any interest in finance she had overnight developed an obsession with investments in every shape and form, in unit trusts, managed funds, gilts, capital bonds, offshore funds, index-linked national savings. She had written to independent financial advisers and bought herself a calculator.

"So how's it all going?" Milly asked, obviously dying of curiosity.

"Splendid thanks. How are you?" Flora asked, ladling tea into the pot. "I'll make some for the rest of them while I'm about it, if you don't mind."

"Oh, we're well and happy. Bobby sees Duncan, of course, and says he seems fine."

"Good."

"Well, he did have a bit of an accident—"

"Oh?" Flora interrupted, alarmed.

"Nothing serious. He just walked into a door and bruised his face and gave himself a black eye. It's easily done, that. But painful. Anything on your face is painful because of all those nerve ends. And of course you can't help being self-conscious, can you? I mean anything on your face makes you feel conspicuous, you think everyone's looking at you, even if they're not. I know because I once bruised my face on a garden rake. Bobby'd left it lying on the grass face upwards, if you see what I mean. And I trod on the prongs, so the handle jumped up and hit me. You should never do that, leave garden tools lying the wrong way up, I mean. So, yes, I do know how painful anything like that can be. But of course the others teased him about it. You know, saying things like, 'You two fighting already are you then?' and so on. Because after all when people have had a punch-up they do sometimes pretend they got a black eye walking into a door, don't they?"

She laughed and then hastily stopped herself, saying, "Not that there's anything funny about it, about their situation, I mean. But you know what men are."

No, I don't, Flora thought. I thought I knew what this particular man was, but I didn't. I got it all wrong.

"Anyway, Bobby says that apart from that little accident, which could happen to anybody, Duncan seems quite his usual self. But of course, he doesn't ask him about anything. And he'd never enquire after Fiona. It wouldn't feel right. Not after knowing you all these years. Everyone in the office feels the same."

"I'm going to take the workers some tea," Flora said, unable to bear this any longer. "Do you want to come and see how they're doing?"

Without waiting for an answer, she took up the tray with mugs of tea and assorted cakes and went ahead.

Nick and Liz had prepared the drawing room thoroughly beforehand, taking out most of the furniture, carefully covering the rest and the carpet. Nick was painting the skirting board and Liz was working on the door. Their grandmother was installed in the middle of the room, sitting in an armchair and wrapped in a dustsheet. Like a baby sitting up in a pram, intrigued with what the adults are doing, she watched her grandchildren with childish delight, peering to see what was going on when their backs were towards her, giggling if anything went wrong. Like Liz, she was wearing a bathcap, which increased the impression of a bonneted baby.

For once Milly Chatterton was at a loss for words.

"She thinks it's better than the telly, don't you, Gran?" Liz said.

Suddenly the spaniel erupted into the room, managing simultaneously to brush the wet skirting board with its tail, push its nose into a tin of paint and lift its leg against the ladder.

"Get it out," Liz and Nick shrieked.

"Oh, naughty Sammy, naughty boy!" Milly exclaimed, waving her hands in the air.

It was Flora who managed to get the dog by the collar and

persuade it and Milly out of the room. Her mother, distracted by the dog, which was even more of a novelty than the decorating, followed them back into the kitchen. Having her with them would at least stop the cross-examination, Flora thought, as she pushed papers aside to make way for the tea things on the table.

Her mother refused the cake and instead began eating cherries which Flora had bought for her that morning.

"One two, buckle my shoe," she said, popping two cherries into her mouth at once, and then spitting the stones out on to her plate.

"Three four, knock at the door." Two more cherries disappeared.

"We used to say that rhyme when we were little," Milly said, watching intrigued.

"Five six, chop up sticks."

"And I still say it to little children to get them to eat. You know how choosey they can be."

"You don't have grandchildren, do you?" Flora asked.

"Seven eight, lay them straight."

"No, not yet. Not much hope either. Our June's a real career girl even though she is living with this man from the gas company and Stanley's that keen on chiropody I don't see him ever getting married."

"Nine ten, a big fat hen."

"It's sad really, I mean I'd love to be a gran. Some people don't like it, do they, they think it makes them seem old, but I'd love it, so I make do by taking little jobs looking after babies and toddlers. And dogs too sometimes."

"I'd no idea you did that."

"Eleven twelve, dig and delve."

"Oh, yes, it's nice to earn a bit of pin money. Not that I *need* to, don't get me wrong. Bobby's always been able to keep his family. I've never had to go out to work, but I enjoy it and it keeps me out of mischief."

"Thirteen fourteen, maids a-courting."

126

"I've just been to see my friend Trudy. Did I ever tell you about my friend Trudy?"

"No, I don't think so."

"Fifteen sixteen, maids in the kitchen."

"Well, it's ever so sad really. They've just parted, her and Basil after, oh I don't know how many years. Twenty maybe. No, it must be twenty-two because I remember they were married just before my mother died and I wore the same coat. I mean it was a good coat and not bright or anything. Navy with paler blue trimming and quite suitable for a funeral really as well as a wedding. I didn't wear the same hat, of course."

"Seventeen eighteen, maids awaiting."

"Well, a couple of years ago Trudy had this little fling with a fellow she hardly knew. It didn't mean anything at all. She meant no harm. It was just that Basil was the only man she'd ever slept with and she wanted to know what it would be like with somebody else. That's all there was to it. But Basil turned very unpleasant and divorced her. She shouldn't have told him."

"Nineteen twenty, my plate's empty."

With a little gesture of triumph, her mother pushed the remains of the cherries away.

"She always goes up to twenty," Flora explained. "And stops."

"Ah, bless her," Milly said, turning affectionately towards the old lady.

"Now, lovey, you could count the stones, couldn't you? Look. This year, next year, sometime, never," she sang out, counting the stones off one by one.

"Silk, satin, cotton, rags," came the rejoinder.

"Well," Milly exclaimed. "There's nothing wrong with your memory, is there?"

The old lady smiled, aware that she had earned some kind of praise.

"Oh, she remembers all kinds of things from her childhood, it's just the immediate memory that's gone."

"Carriage, coach," Milly began.

"Wheelbarrow, muckcart," the old lady supplied triumphantly.

"Do you like games, like card games?" Milly asked.

She nodded.

"I've got some special games at home. I could bring some to play with you."

"What sort of games?" Flora asked.

"Oh, you know very simple ones. I find if I'm looking after an old lady or gentleman they play the same sort of games as little children. Easy jigsaws too, they like those. But they can't concentrate for long, just like children."

"Tinker, tailor, soldier, spy."

"That's right, Gran. Oh, you're a quick one, you are," Milly told her.

She looked at the clock.

"Goodness, is that the time? Bobby'll be in soon and I've nothing ready."

"And Nick should be getting off to work," Flora said, getting up.

"Oh look, your mum doesn't want me to go," Milly said.

It was true; Flora could see that her mother was pouting with disapproval.

"Don't you worry, lovey," Milly said, stooping to kiss the old lady on the cheek. "I'll come back and see you tomorrow. Is that all right, Flora? I'll bring some games."

Flora was looking thoughtfully at the two of them.

"Yes, of course," she said. "It would be lovely to see you again, Milly."

Seventeen

"The offer is quite unacceptable," Flora said firmly. "I've calculated that the most that sum would bring in, if safely invested, would be fifty-six pounds a week."

Mr Coffey nodded his agreement; instinct told her that he'd thought this all along but had wanted her to make up her own mind.

"So you are instructing me to reject the proposal?" he asked.

"Yes."

"Then we must come up with a counter-proposal. I suggest you prepare a list of all your expenses, everything you need for yourself, the children, the house. Some, like the fuel bills, will be obvious, but remember to allow for household repairs, decorating, replacement of clothes, holidays. And have you thought about the matter of university fees?"

"Yes. I've made an appointment to see them again. In fact I'm going over to County Hall after I've left you."

"Good." He smiled approvingly. "I see you have it all in hand, but don't hesitate to ring if there is anything you're unsure about. I'll tell your husband's solicitors that the offer is unacceptable and drop you a line the minute I have a reply from them."

What a difference, he thought after she had left him, between this woman as she was now and as she had been when she crept nervously into his office two months ago. She'd seemed ready then to accept anything her husband threw at her. Now she was rejecting his proposal with all the conviction of a union leader turning down a pay offer. Any moment now she'd be calling it derisory.

Time was all she had needed, he reflected, time to adjust and prepare. He should have realised that, for had he not often observed that women can summon up reserves of patience and endurance to bear anything? It is the sudden shock, the unexpected blow which overwhelms them.

Flora too was pleased with herself as she set off for County Hall, thirty miles away. Her last interview here had been just after Liz had had her university place confirmed. Assessed on Duncan's income, they would have had no help with the fees and the loan entitlement would have been quite small, though the fact that there were two of them studying at the same time had increased it. The situation was quite different now and she was prepared to do battle to prove it.

She looked at her notes and practised what she would say as she had a sandwich lunch in a coffee bar to fill in time before her appointment with Miss Scarr, the officer in charge of student loans, who had dealt with her before.

She was a very confident young woman, this Miss Scarr, she remembered; one of those successful modern career women with challenging eyes, smart suits and aggressive shoulders. Fiona from Publicity was probably similar, Flora thought as she went in to her office.

All the same, she wasn't going to be put down by her, she resolved as she launched into her prepared spiel, outlining what had happened, concluding with, "So you see we shouldn't now be assessed on my husband's income, but on my own which is currently being negotiated, the last figure on offer being fifty-six pounds a week."

"I'm very sorry to hear this," Miss Scarr said, sounding unexpectedly sympathetic. "Of course, everything will have to be reassessed in view of your changed circumstances. Fees will be paid for you if your income is below ten thousand pounds a year and a seventy-five per cent loan allowed. But of course we would need proof of your income, so you must keep in touch with us and let us know regularly what your current income is, with documentation to prove it so that we can assess what support we can give Liz and Nick. I'm sorry that we have to ask you to do that when you have so much to worry about just now, but it really is the only way we can do our best for you."

To be given such sympathy, when she'd expected an argument, had her nonplussed for a moment. And the way this stranger had said the children's names, that touched her too. She drove home feeling happier than she had done since Duncan's abrupt departure out of her life.

Nick and Liz were hard at work painting the woodwork in the dining room.

"How did you get on, Mum?" Liz asked, putting down the paint brush.

"Fine, darling. Mr Coffey agrees we should turn down your father's offer, so we shall wait and see what ensues. Then at County Hall they were really helpful. If you need a full grant for your fees, you'll get it. Of course it won't come to that, but it's such a relief to have a safety net. Yes, it's been a good day."

"We've been thinking, Liz and I," Nick said, "that really it's a bit pointless having a dining room we hardly ever use. Why don't you have this as a study? It's a much better size and far brighter than that gloomy little pokehole you and Dad called a study."

It was true; it was really only on high days and holidays and when they were having guests for dinner that they used this room, which was inconveniently placed at the other end of the house from the kitchen. And there wouldn't be dinner parties any more with Duncan gone. Kitchen friends, that's what she'd have now.

"You could move your desk from the hall over to the alcove on the right of the fireplace and you need another bookcase anyway, so it could go in the alcove on the left of the fireplace," Nick went on.

"And I hope you don't mind, but we looked in that filing

cabinet of Dad's in the spare room and he's emptied everything out of it, all his files and so on, so we could bring it down
here for you. You'll need all that kind of office equipment
when you start work properly in the autumn."

"Thank you. It's lovely of you both."

She didn't mean that all this rearranging of furniture was
lovely; it was their concern for her that moved her; she'd
always assumed that she was the one to do the caring.

"And we've thought of something else too, Mum. For your
bedroom."

"What's that?"

"Come along up and we'll show you."

"You go, Liz. I want to get the rest of this door done or it'll
go streaky."

So Liz and Flora went upstairs together and stood in the
doorway of the transformed bedroom, now much brighter
with its white paintwork and walls emulsioned in some colour
she could never remember the name of, but which had the
slightest touch of warm pink about it.

"We thought we could move Dad's old compactum out into
the spare room and bring in here the wardrobe that's in there.
It's much the best one in the house and why waste it on the
occasional guest when you could use it every day?"

"Where will it go?"

"We've measured it and reckon it'll fit exactly into that
alcove by the chimney breast. In fact we think it'll look like a
fitted cupboard."

"It's a wonderful idea," Flora began, turning to her daughter.

Something barrel-shaped and hairy shuffled into the room
behind her.

"My God, what's that?"

Liz laughed.

"It's called Miss Sukie and Milly Chatterton brought it with
her when she came round. She's looking after it for a friend.
Just for the day, thank goodness. That foul spaniel did

another poo on the lawn. Gran trod on it and then walked it into the kitchen."

"Oh, no, the smell'll be awful."

"It's OK, don't panic. I cleared it up and flung evil-smelling disinfectant all over the place."

"So Milly's here? I didn't see the car."

"She took it round the back. She's in the garden now with Gran. Gran's as happy as a flea with Milly, so I suppose we have to forgive the dogs."

"I'll go and have a word."

She went downstairs, the peke lolloping behind her, almost too fat to walk.

Gran and Milly were circling the orchard, arm in arm.

"Round and round the garden," she heard Milly intoning as she approached. "Like a teddy bear. One step, two step and—"

And Gran was already giggling in anticipation, remembering that once, years ago, tickling had ensued.

"Oh, we get on like a house on fire, your mum and me, don't we lovey? We played jigsaws and did a bit of hide and seek in the orchard. How are you, Flora dear? I hope you don't mind me popping in like this after lunch? I did promise to bring the games. Where's that dog gone?"

Flora shrugged. When last seen the spaniel had been digging up her baby carrots and bouncing on a row of lettuces. Since he was impervious to orders, there didn't seem much point in saying anything to Milly about it.

"His owners are coming back at the weekend and I must say I won't be sorry. Give me a baby or an oldie to look after any day. I like dogs, don't get me wrong, but he's that destructive, we've had to put him into the garage at nights, but he howls and the neighbours complain."

She paused for breath and then went on, "Mind you, hamsters can be difficult too. We had to look after one that escaped and used to come back at night and chew the curtains. We couldn't catch it. In the end Bobby had to put a trap down and get it that way. Then of course we had to take its body to the pet shop to try and match it up. The owners never knew. And of course we never let on. Still, not as bad as my friend Paula who was looking after a friend's chihuahua and the cat ate it. Thought it was a rat, you see. Well, you can't blame the cat, can you? I mean they do look like little rats, don't you think? Mind you, it was a spiteful cat. It got the goldfish the week after. At least that spaniel looks like a real dog even if it does jump about and tear things up. Come on Sukie, time to go home."

"Milly, are you looking after pets and babies and oldies all this summer?"

"Goodness, bless you no. I've nothing booked up for a while. I couldn't do it nonstop. The house gets in such a pickle and Bobby likes things nice and tidy. And—"

"I was wondering if you'd be interested in helping to care for Gran, as a proper job, I mean, when I start work in the autumn? She's all right for spells on her own, she doesn't wander, but she gets fed up. There's a Mrs Herbert comes in first thing and cleans her flat and doesn't mind staying to keep her company—"

"Of course I'll help out. I'd like that. She's no trouble and I'll tell you something: I hate being on my own. I've always hated my own company. I used to like it where we lived when the children were little and we were always popping in and out of each other's houses."

They made their way very slowly up towards the house, Gran hanging on to Milly's arm and the peke staggering along behind, its tongue falling out of the side of its mouth and its lead trailing behind it. The spaniel tore across the vegetable plot and dashed past them, tossing a look of total canine contempt at the peke as it did so.

Nick and Liz had brought a tray of tea out on to the patio.

"We thought you'd like a cup before you go," Liz said, rather pointedly, her mother thought.

"Well, I won't say no," Milly said, sitting down, the peke alongside.

"I'm not working on Thursday night, Mum," Nick said. "They don't need me. I could have changed to a day shift, but it's not worth altering just for the one off. And I must say it'll be great to have all Friday to paint and not have to spend the morning sleeping."

His mother smiled, remembering the time not so long ago when he was quite happy to spend all the morning sleeping.

"And I'm free on Friday too," Liz put in. "Violet has to go into hospital for tests. Just routine, but it means no lessons."

"That's a pretty name, Violet," Milly said, helping herself to more cake and then feeding little bits of it to the fat peke.

"Why don't you both take the day off and enjoy yourselves for a change?"

"No, we reckon we could just about do the hall in one day, both working flat out. There isn't much furniture to move."

"There are five doors –" Liz pointed out.

"Six. You've forgotten the cloakroom. But, anyway, Mum, we *do* enjoy it, don't we, Liz?"

"Yes," she agreed, rather less enthusiastically. "Though I must say that if I never paint a panelled door again, I shan't exactly grieve about it."

The peke, which had been scratching itself, now took to snuffling its undercarriage.

"Stop that, Sukie," Milly said. "It's very rude. I can't stop her," she apologised to the others. "She's always licking her naughty bits."

Flora saw Liz and Nick exchange glances, heard the intake of breath which was a prelude to helpless laughter. She got up to distract Milly with the offer of more tea.

At that moment the spaniel, unable to bear the sight of the peke any longer, picked up the end of the lead in its teeth and set off across the garden. The astonished peke was obliged to stagger along behind. The spaniel accelerated. So, perforce, did the peke. The spaniel ran up the bank by the rockery, dragging the other up too, then suddenly rushed down again. The peke followed, rolling over and over in a blurred furry bundle.

The spaniel was barking furiously by this time and Milly was shrieking at them both. Nick set off in pursuit, while Liz lay back in her chair and gave herself up to uncontrolled laughter. The excitement was too much for her grandmother, who keeled gently over on to the grass, knocking the table over as she did so.

Eighteen

W as it really three months since Duncan had gone? Flora wondered, looking down her July garden and remembering that day in early April when they had sat here having breakfast together for the last time.

Now the three of them were sitting here on the same patio, breakfast on the same table, just as it had been then – except that everything was different. Sometimes it seemed like yesterday, sometimes it might have been a lifetime away. Sometimes she was plunged in despair, sometimes she felt strong and able to count her blessings. This morning was one of the better times.

The children had been great, she never would have believed it of them. The house, thanks to them, was so much lighter and fresher. Still the same familiar place, of course, but somehow more cheerful. The garden was looking lovely and that nice Mr Woodcock, who came around now and then, had said he would take over the Atco when Nick went.

She could bear to think about the future now; it no longer seemed to stretch ahead of her, dark and threatening and herself a lonely figure in its hostile landscape, lost and frightened. She no longer shied away from the very prospect of it; there was interest ahead now and hope. There was to be work there, colleagues and friends, sometimes her children, always her home and garden. It would be a different future certainly, from what she had for years taken for granted it would be with Duncan, but it had begun to seem possible that it might be equally good.

Liz laughed suddenly.

"What is it?"

Liz shook her head.

"Nothing. It's just that every now and then I think of Milly with her naughty bits and then the dog dragging the peke all over the garden and then Gran sending the tea things flying and it hits me again and I just have to laugh."

"Yes, it was very funny. But she could have hurt herself, you know."

"Well, you did get the doctor to check, Mum, and he said she was a tough old bird."

"He didn't put it quite like that, Liz."

"After she'd wagged her finger at him and said, 'Don't you touch me. I know your sort,' he probably felt like saying something much worse."

"Time we made a start on the hall, Liz," Nick said, draining his cup of coffee.

"One day," Flora said suddenly, "I'll repay you both for everything you've done since your father left."

"Don't be silly, Mum. You already have."

"I can't get over how incredibly quick you've been with the decorating. When we used to decorate, your father and I, it used to take us weeks to do just one room."

"That was because of all the preparing he used to do, all that filling in and rubbing down, every tiny crack stuffed with Polyfilla and left to dry overnight. Life's too short. And afterwards there's nearly always a wardrobe or bookcase in front so nobody sees the imperfections anyway."

"Quick, cheap and nasty, that's us," Liz told her.

"But clean with it," Nick pointed out. "I'll start putting the dustsheets down in the hall, Liz. You finish your coffee."

He came back with the post.

"I thought there wasn't any this morning," his mother said, holding out her hand.

"Oh, don't think the cellophane-wrapped brigade would

forget you, Mum. Here's *Renovations, Future Times* and *Highland Plastics*. And one proper letter."

Flora dropped the magazines and opened the letter. They saw her expression change.

"Oh, no," she said. "No."

"What is it, Mum?"

"He's said, he's said," her voice broke and for a moment she couldn't go on. "He's said he wants to sell this house."

"He can't."

"He's instructed his solicitor to say he wants it sold and the money divided. He says it's too big for me now."

"What a bloody cheek! Just because he's gone. Can I see, Mum?"

"Just let me finish it. There you are, Liz."

Everything to be taken from her, everything smashed, the garden they'd toiled in all these years, the house the children had just decorated with so much love. Her home, her secure place. It was too cruel, tears pricked her eyes.

He called it an asset. He had become one of those people who think of a house as an asset, who don't understand what a home means. And he'd said that the children didn't need it any more now that they were grown up, that they'd soon have places of their own. It was all very well for the childless to think like that, but he was a parent, he should know how much they still needed their home, a home to leave, a home to come back to.

"Mr Coffey says in his letter that you can go and see him as soon as possible, Mum. Shall I ring for an appointment for you?"

"No, I'll go," she said, surreptitiously rubbing her forefinger across her cheek to wipe away the tears. To think that only minutes ago she was cheerfully looking forward to the future! Whom the gods wish to destroy they don't need to drive mad, just make over-confident.

"A cuppa before you go in, Mum?"

"No, thanks, darling. Maybe afterwards."

139

"My God, I could kill that father of ours," Liz said, when her mother was out of earshot. "What the hell does he think he's playing at?"

"He wants the money. That's all he cares about now. He wants the money so he can live somewhere nice with Fiona from Publicity."

"He can't make Mum sell it, can he?"

"The solicitor will know. I don't. The last thing she needs now is to face a move. She's coping bloody well, but I reckon that would be more than she could take."

"I suppose we could buy him out. He says he wants to have it valued. If we could find half the money it's valued at . . ."

"It's not the sort of money you raise coaching kids and filling superstore shelves, Liz."

"No."

"She's being a long time. Do you think she can't get through?"

"More likely she's gone to tidy herself up, you know how she always likes to put on a brave face for us. Sh, she's coming."

"Any luck for an appointment soon, Mum?"

"Yes, Liz. I only spoke to his secretary, and she said he was fully booked today and Monday, but she'd have a word with him and apparently he said he knew I'd be worried so he'd see me after his last client tonight at about five thirty."

"You're going out to supper with the Pattersons tonight, aren't you?"

"Maybe I'll cancel."

"No, you go. It'll do you good. And they're old friends, not the sort you have to be all formal with. I'll see to Gran."

"Thanks, Liz. Yes. I'll go straight on in that case, they're in Bloxfield too. Oh, what about the car for you to get to work, Nick?"

"That's all right. I'll cycle."

"Lights OK?"

"Yes, I saw to them last week. Come on, Liz, we might as well get on with it."

140

It seemed a long, dreary day to all of them. The fun had gone out of the decorating.

"Maybe we're doing it for someone else?" Liz said. "And they'd probably redecorate anyway. People do. I can't bear the thought of someone else living here."

"Let's not think about it. And I think we should start on the outside tomorrow, like we planned.

"What's the point now?"

"Well, if it *is* sold, people will pay more if the outside looks good."

"I don't see why we should slave away so our bloody father can get more money for our house."

"Half of it would go to Mum," Nick reminded her.

"I suppose so," Liz agreed without enthusiasm.

So they worked in silence, trying not to think of what lay ahead.

Flora cleared the dishes, put a few things ready for lunch and went upstairs to the flat.

"Never see you nowadays," her mother greeted her gloomily.

"Oh, yes, you do. I brought your breakfast up not long ago."

"Was that you? I thought it was the maid."

"No, it was me."

Her mother looked about her, lowered her voice and said, "They're putting something in the food. Her with those two things told me."

"Milly? With the peke and the spaniel?"

"Yes, Spaniards."

"You like her, don't you?"

"I'd rather have cherries," said her mother, who never cared to admit to liking anyone.

They played patience and did a jigsaw and the endless morning dragged on. Lunch was a dreary meal, everyone trying to be cheerful for everyone else's sake and nobody quite succeeding.

In the afternoon she went out and did some gardening while her mother slept in the hammock. She's shrinking, Flora thought, she looks like a child curled up in there. The ground was dry, the recent rain didn't seem to have had much effect on the soil. Good hoeing weather, she thought as she worked between the rows in the vegetable plot, picking up carrots which Milly's spaniel had dug up, pushing others back into the soil.

She wandered over to the flower beds, snipping off dead heads; the roses were easy enough but the pansies involved a lot of bending and her back was soon aching. She sat down, disconsolate. The garden was looking too lovely; it hurt to think of leaving it. Try not to think about anything until after the interview with Mr Coffey. Time now to start thinking of the family's evening meal, getting Nick off to work, getting her mother ready for the night.

"I've brought the figures you asked me for," she told Mr Coffey that evening.

The little west-facing room was warm with the heat of the long day. Mr Coffey was, she thought, looking tired. She was grateful to him for staying, when he'd probably much rather be at home, having a drink in his garden.

"I'd prepared them all before this bombshell about selling the house," she explained. "I don't know how relevant they are now."

"Good, they're still relevant."

He took them from her.

"I take it you want to stay where you are?"

"Oh, yes. It's my home."

He caught the edge of panic in her voice.

"He can't force you out," he said. "But it is quite usual to sell the matrimonial home, so don't worry, it's natural they should suggest it. But what we must go for is a settlement which leaves you the house plus a reasonable share of his income and of course your joint savings."

She shook her head.

"We don't have any capital," she said. "Just a very little each in building societies. You know how it is when the children are growing up, you can't save much."

"You're sure he hasn't anything hidden away? It does happen, I'm afraid."

"No, I'd have known. We shared everything like that."

"The house will have to be valued, not for sale, but because he'll want to know how much it's worth as part of the settlement. Any idea of its value?"

"It's quite an ordinary little house," she told him. "What's special about it is the unusually large amount of land that goes with it. That's what made us buy it all those years ago, that and the big kitchen. But of course some people nowadays don't want a big garden. So," she admitted, shaking her head, "I honestly don't know what the house is worth."

"It's usually more than one thinks," he said, smiling.

Somebody else recently had said that about a house; it had been bought for a couple of thousand and was now worth hundreds of thousands. Who was it? Of course, it was Duncan's parents, she remembered suddenly. They'd said it of Duncan's aunt who was leaving him all her money. Of course, his aunt had assumed that it would go to her and the children as well, but it wouldn't now. He had it. When he offered her that measly fifty-six pounds a week, he'd had over two hundred thousands pounds in the bank. If not more, because that was only the house.

Mr Coffey was repeating something he'd already said.

"I'm sorry, but I've just thought of something that might be important," she told him.

He listened carefully.

"It's strange that his solicitors haven't mentioned this in their letter of voluntary disclosure," he said. "I shall write to them again specifically about this inheritance and I'll obtain a copy of your husband's aunt's will to find out exactly what it says. As soon as it's available I'll request a copy of the Grant of Probate. Then I suggest that we spend two or three hundred pounds to take barrister's opinion about your entitlement."

He paused, as if giving her time to take this in, and then went on, "I'm sorry to say that if your husband has deliberately withheld information about the inheritance then we may have a fight on our hands."

She thought about it, sitting there in his warm office, the sun shining directly on to them through the west-facing window. She knew it was one of those moments of decision, knew that she couldn't go on living with so much uncertainty. She steeled herself to agree.

"I might have to advise court proceedings if we find that your husband has not been forthcoming about all his assets and/or he is not prepared to increase his offer."

Take Duncan to court! She tried to think calmly about Mr Coffey's words, but the thought of a court case, of taking on these powerful people, appalled her. It wasn't just the thought of the expense, if Duncan went back on his promise to pay her legal bills, which he might do if barristers were involved; it was the aggressiveness of it which frightened her. This wasn't her world. She'd never been a fighter. To defend yourself and your children was one thing, but to go into the attack was quite another.

"Can I have a little time to think about it?" she asked.

"Of course," he said. "It has to be your decision entirely."

He smiled as they shook hands, but she had a feeling that he was disappointed in her, had thought she was made of sterner stuff.

Nineteen

"There, Gran, that's the lot. Now for your tablets," Liz said.

"They're not aphrodisiacs but they do help me sleep," her grandmother told her knowledgeably.

It was one of those child-proof containers that only children seem able to open. Liz got the hang of it at last and took out two tablets.

"One two, buckle my shoe," her grandmother said, almost singing the words, as she popped the tablets into her mouth.

"Take plenty of water with them," Liz told her, handing her the glass.

Like a child, Gran did as she was told.

"I'll take the dishes down, Gran, and bring you back your hot drink," Liz told her as she put the lid back on. "Mum's gone out to dinner with the Pattersons but she says she'll pop in to see you when she gets home."

"Who's she?" Gran asked.

"Your daughter."

"Oh, yes, of course, she had the grocer's shop in the village."

"Shan't be long, Gran."

It must be awful for Mum, she thought, as she ran the dishes under the tap, then, remembering Nick, hastily put in the plug. It's bad enough for me, but for her own daughter to see her like this. What would I do if Mum went the same way? I wouldn't want to see it. I'd rather she just died suddenly. Then the thought of her mother not being there, not being there to

145

turn to, talk to, get advice from, even if only to ignore it, was so awful that her tears began to plop into the washing-up water.

She sniffed, blew her nose and put the mug of milk into the microwave, and stood watching it go round as she tried not to think of life without her mother. But often nowadays this fear of her mother's death overwhelmed her. It was as if she could no longer take her presence for granted since her father had disappeared out of her life.

She wondered how her mother had got on with Mr Coffey. She'd had a tiny hope that perhaps she'd ring afterwards and say it was all a mistake, what he'd said in his letter about selling their home. But she hadn't. She looked around her at all the familiar things; it just seemed so bizarre to think of the house divided in two, half his and half hers and of having to buy his half. There had to be a way out, a way of getting hold of lots of money.

She measured the Ovaltine into the milk, stirred it and carried it back into her grandmother's bedroom.

Her grandmother was sitting by the window where she had left her. She had contrived to get the top off the tablets and had spread them across the little table. She was crooning to herself.

"Three four, knock at the door," she sang, popping two more tablets into her mouth, taking up the glass and drinking.

"Five six, chop up sticks," she chanted, popping two more of the dangerous little pills into her mouth and reaching for the glass.

Liz watched her, for a moment so horrified that she couldn't move, then, knowing she must act quickly, drew in her breath to shout.

Suddenly she stopped herself.

What was the point of saving her grandmother's life? What sort of life was it? She didn't know who she was, or who her own daughter was. If something happened to her, like an accidental overdose, wouldn't it be for the best? Maybe her

Gran, in some unconscious way, was seeking to end her own life. Who was she to frustrate her? What right had she to interfere?

And if her Gran died, Mum would have the money, money enough to buy Dad's share of the house, so they could all stay here. If Gran had been in her right mind, wouldn't she have wanted that? Wouldn't any mother trade in her own useless life to help her daughter and her grandchildren? It's what Flora would have done for her and Nick.

It wasn't like murder, she thought, it wasn't as if she was deliberately doing anything to hurt her grandmother. It was Gran who was happily plying herself with tablets and she'd go on like this, she knew she would, right up to nineteen twenty, my plate's empty. She was into the rhythm of it now. Why stop her?

"Seven eight, lay them straight."

She dashed forward.

"No, Gran, you mustn't. It's dangerous. Oh, how wicked I was. I'm sorry, Gran. Please, forgive me, please."

She was crying, scooping up the tablets, pouring them back into the jar, horrified at herself.

Her Gran was laughing.

"It's a new game," she said. "I like it. Who are you? Would you like a sweet?"

"I must telephone, Gran."

"That's nice."

"She's taken six of them instead of two," she told the hospital doctor, after reading the name of the tablets off the container.

He was reassuring.

"Six won't hurt, though she may be a bit drowsy. She'd have to take at least twelve before there was any cause for anxiety. Nothing under twenty would be fatal. There's nothing to worry about as long as she doesn't have any other symptoms. So keep an eye on her and of course if you're worried, bring her in."

She was shaking as she put the receiver down, her voice trembled as she asked, "Shall we play patience, Gran?"

"Mm, but I liked that game with the little sweeties."

"No," Liz told her. "No more of that until tomorrow."

She got out the cards and dealt them. Her grandmother watched with childish delight as the pile in front of her grew. Avidly, she turned them over to see what she'd got, then suddenly bored, turned them face down again, only to pick them up when something sparked her interest.

For the next hour they sat together, Liz watching anxiously as her grandmother played around with the cards, put them on top of each other, occasionally matching them in pairs. Even Snap was beyond her now. So Liz built her a house of cards, which her grandmother loved to knock over when she'd finished, just like I used to knock over sandcastles which Dad built, Liz remembered.

Gran's all right, she thought, there's no need to tell Mum what happened.

At ten o'clock, Flora came up.

The minute she saw her, Liz knew that she couldn't keep it from her.

"We nearly had an accident, Mum. She managed to get the top off the tablets while I was getting her Ovaltine."

"Oh, no! How many did she take?"

"Six altogether, that's counting the two she was meant to have. I rang the hospital and they said there was nothing to worry about, so long as she didn't have any other symptoms."

"Oh, well done, darling. You've coped marvellously. No, six wouldn't hurt, but you must have got an awful fright. I'll take over now, you look very tired," and her eyes raked her daughter's face, in that familiar anxious way.

They hugged each other and for a moment Liz clung to her mother, guiltily aware that she had told her the truth, but not the whole truth.

Twenty

"Tell us all about it, Mum," they pressed her over an early breakfast the next morning.

Nick had stayed up after work just to know what had happened.

She told them, explaining that she only knew about their great aunt's money by hearsay.

"Ring up the grandparents and ask them."

"It's awfully awkward, Liz. They must know by now that Dad's gone, but they haven't rung or written."

"Won't they think it's odd that you haven't? I mean you were always ringing them before, much more than Dad ever did."

"I know it's what you've wanted me to do all along and I've thought about it. At first I just didn't want to upset them, then well, you know how it is if you leave something; time passes and you just never get round to it."

"Like not writing thank you letters and then it gets too late," suggested Nick, for whom that fearful chore had cast a shadow over childhood Christmases and birthdays.

"Something like that. I seem to remember a certain amount of persuasion was required in your case."

"Persuasion! It was downright bullying. You used to stand over me hour after hour."

"Poor old Nick," she said, laughing and rumpling his hair. "You ought to get off to bed. You look exhausted."

"Work did seem to go on and on last night," he agreed, getting up, stretching and yawning. "I expect I'd got out of the way of it, after having a day off."

149

"Have a bath, it'll relax you."

"All right, but I'll leave the water in so we can use it for the garden. Could you take it down in buckets, Liz, when it's cooled?"

"No, you can take it yourself."

"I've been thinking, I could rig up a hosepipe from the bath and out of the window. Water finds its own level so it would go down to the ground and we could collect it in a barrel down there. I was looking at the meter under the sink yesterday and it was whizzing round."

"Don't worry about it now. Just go to bed."

"So Mr Coffey doesn't think Dad can make us leave?" Liz asked after her brother had departed.

"Well, I can't swear to that, darling. I mean it might be the only way we could keep a roof over our heads. The idea would be that with half the money from this house we could get some little place – oh, my God, what about Mother? How was it I hadn't thought of it before? She'll never settle and we wouldn't have room to make her a flat."

"Then she'd have to go into the home."

"I wonder . . ."

"What?"

"I think I'm going to consult her Mr Hardcastle."

She wrote to Mr Hardcastle setting out the situation in detail, explaining that her mother was still very physically fit and able to live at home, but that the flat was under threat as her husband now wanted to sell the house of which it was a part. Would it be possible to use any of her mother's funds, she asked, up to the value of the flat, to contribute to the cost of buying out her share of the house?

Mr Hardcastle replied suggesting a date when he might come down and talk to her and also see her mother so that he could judge for himself what her state of health required.

"The first thing you'll notice about him when he comes tomorrow," she warned Liz, "is that he's very, very correct."

"A manners maketh man, sort of man?"

"Right."

"In other words you're asking me to behave myself, watch my tongue and all that?"

"Right again."

"Good old Mum. I'll be a credit to you. How shall we play it? You'll talk to him first in your newly painted study, then go upstairs to Gran and I'll bring up some tea for the three of you and bugger off sharpish."

Mr Hardcastle was tall and very upright. He walked like a military man, and wore his dark suit like a uniform. His shoes shone, his hair was carefully brushed, he carried a brief case and an umbrella although the weather clearly didn't have rain in mind.

All this Liz observed, as she watched from her bedroom as he got out of his car and walked towards the front door.

Her mother answered the door. Once he was safely in the study Liz went downstairs and into the kitchen to prepare the tea.

Her plan was different from her mother's. It seemed to her that much the best thing was for Mr Hardcastle to pay for Gran to go into the home. That way her mother could go to work without anxiety and without the need of having Milly Chatterton and her menagerie taking up semi-residence. She knew, however, that it wasn't just a question of money. Mr Hardcastle would have to be convinced that Gran should be in a home, that she wasn't really fit to live like this any more. She didn't want him to see Gran at her best. To be blunt she wanted him to see Gran at her very worst.

She began by making egg sandwiches. Gran hated eggs and was inclined to petulance if one hove into view. An egg sandwich was the kind of thing she might pick up and squeeze resentfully until it oozed between her fingers. Not the sort of thing that would appeal to the fastidious Mr Hardcastle. Liz put three eggs on to boil and began slicing a white loaf because Gran preferred brown.

So far so good. She'd thought long and hard about what might be the messiest sort of cake to offer for tea and had cycled into the town and bought meringues. Of course Mum had already baked a Victoria sponge and some rock buns, but she reckoned meringues would catch Gran's eye as being something of a novelty. And soon they would catch the rest of her face because she wasn't exactly a tidy eater nowadays.

As for the tea itself, Gran liked hers good and strong, a deep orange-brown colour. So Liz decided she'd make a pot of very weak china tea and serve it with slices of lemon. Her mother liked it like that and Mr Hardcastle looked as if he might. With a bit of luck, Gran would call it gnat's pee and tip it into a flower pot.

At four o'clock she went upstairs to the flat and tapped at the door.

"Ready for tea?" she asked politely.

"Come in, Liz, and meet Mr Hardcastle," her mother said.

She shook hands and when he said, "How do you do?" resisted the temptation to say, "How do I do what?" and just shook hands politely and said she'd bring the tea up.

"Aren't you having any, darling?" her mother asked, surprised at there being only three cups.

"No, you have things to discuss," she said, carefully placing egg sandwiches and meringues within Gran's reach. She was tempted all the same; she'd like to see the po-faced Mr Hardcastle's reaction when Gran erupted.

It seemed a long time before she heard her mother and Mr Hardcastle come downstairs, heard sounds of polite farewells and of his car driving away.

Her mother came into the kitchen, looking cheerful.

"Well, that went very well," she said. "Thanks for all your help, darling."

"Did Gran enjoy her tea?"

Her mother looked surprised.

"Yes, I'm sure she did. She enjoyed the sandwiches, though I'm afraid she called them chicken paste. She didn't touch the meringues, but it was a very kind thought of yours. And she loved the lemon tea."

Kind thought indeed, Liz muttered to herself as she went upstairs to help bring down the tea things.

"Tell me what he said," she asked her mother as they washed up.

"Well, darling, he was really very helpful and understanding. He could quite see that Gran needs to stay in her flat and seems to think that her funds can be used to secure her a home here with us. As he said, the money has to be administered in her best interests and her best interest is to stay here."

"But it's no good just buying out the flat, is it, without the house around it?" Liz said, still feeling gloomy at the failure of her plans. "I mean he'll have to fork out more than just the value of the flat, won't he, if we're to stay?"

"Exactly. And that's what needs to be worked out. But it's a good first step."

"And then, even if you're allowed to keep the house, we still need money to run it. I do think you ought to ring up the other grandparents."

"Yes, you're right. I've thought about it and I'm going to ring this evening. They might be ill or anything and Duncan wouldn't have let me know."

Her father-in-law answered the phone.

"It's good to hear from you, Flora. I'll get Mother."

So he's opted out pretty quickly, Flora thought as she held the line. There was a long delay in which she imagined them having a whispered discussion of what to say to her. At last her mother-in-law came to the phone.

"Well, how are you, Flora? And the children? You're all well?"

"Yes, thank you, Ma. And you?"

"Oh, we're not too bad, Father and me."

"I'm sorry I haven't rung for so long, Ma. I've been a bit – distracted."

Give her a chance to say she knows why.

"Have you? Well, everyone's very busy nowadays, aren't they?"

This could go on for ever. So much for blunt Northerners. She, Southern Flora, would have to be the blunt one.

"Duncan has left me. Did you know that?"

There was a pause, then the cautious reply, "Well, yes, we had heard. Our Duncan informed us. We were sorry to hear of it, Father and I."

Our Duncan, she noted.

"We were shocked too, Ma, me and the children."

"I can imagine. But it's what your generation does nowadays, isn't it? We just have to accept it. Times have changed. Father and I realise that."

The conversation was shrivelling. Dried bits of non-communication on the line.

"Well, thank you for ringing, Flora. Father sends his love. And to the children, of course. We won't forget them at Christmas."

She put the receiver down and sat, stunned.

How could she – Ma, who had always seemed so fond of them all, not just of the children, but of herself too? This change in her was almost as much of a shock as Duncan's betrayal. Yes, she felt betrayed by his parents.

She tried to put herself in Ma's position. If, in twenty years' time, Nick told her that his marriage had broken up, would she, Flora, be truly concerned about his ex-wife? Wouldn't Nick always be the one who counted? Flesh of her flesh? A daughter-in-law, however much liked, was still only a daughter-in-law.

Not wanting Liz to see her in this state of despair, she slipped quietly out into the garden, down through the orchard and settled herself in that rough little corner, by the compost heap, which caught the last of the evening sun. The grass was long here but so dry that it made a rasping sound as she sat down, her legs stretched out in front of her; the brick wall, which had absorbed the heat of the day, was warm against her back.

Before the call she had thought it likely that all of Aunt Mabel's money would go to Duncan. Now she was sure of it. It would furnish his luxury love nest with Fiona from Publicity and give them exotic holidays in faraway places.

Not if she could prevent it, it wouldn't, she thought with sudden rage. It wasn't what Aunt Mabel had intended when she left her fortune to her nephew. She had meant it for all of them and it was her duty now to see that Aunt Mabel's wish was carried out.

She had always been too accepting of her lot, she thought with sudden self-contempt. She hadn't objected to being dumped in a boarding school or in other people's houses as she should have done. She hadn't fought back at her mother, when her mother was in her prime, she hadn't fought to keep David. And now, here she was, accepting Duncan's parents' view of things, forgiving them because it's human nature to side with your own flesh and blood. She wasn't a fighter, that was her trouble.

And then she remembered the ducklings.

Years ago, when the children were quite small, they had stayed in a cottage in Devon, taking Duncan's parents with them. The cottage had a long overgrown garden at the bottom of which was a field with a pond. A mother duck had recently hatched her eggs and they used to watch, leaning on the fence, as she helped them out of the water and proudly marched them in a line across the field and back. Liz and Nick, of course, always wanted to go in and play with them, but she wouldn't let them.

"It would frighten her," she said. "Think how big you'd seem to her."

One evening as the six of them leaned on the fence and watched the little procession of fluffy ducklings leave the water

155

and start across the field, they saw, to their horror, a bulldog run out from one of the cottages on the far side of the pond and dash towards the ducklings, barking and growling. The mother duck, who a moment ago had seemed so big compared with her little ones, now looked tiny and vulnerable.

The children screamed.

"Save them," they shrieked as the adults stood helpless, knowing there was no time to get between the dog and the ducks, though Duncan did grab a stick and make for the gate into the field.

Suddenly the mother duck turned, swung round to face the dog, and, her wings outspread, running on the tips of her feet, her neck outstretched, made straight for him. Flora remembered shutting her eyes so that she wouldn't see the great barrel-chested dog snap that neck in two, rip the brave little body open.

When she opened them, the dog was scampering away, tail between its legs, back to the cottage and the duck was leading her family back to the safety of the pond.

They had stood, the six of them, dumbfounded.

"Well, would you believe that?" Pa had said at last. "I've never seen the like."

"It's a wonderful thing is nature," his wife told him. "The way she turned on him!"

"But she must have known she hadn't a chance. One snap and he'd have done for her."

"But she didn't stop to work that out," Ma had told him. "She reacted by instinct, as mothers should."

That was a voice from the past all right, she thought as she sat down here by the compost heap, but she could still hear it quite distinctly. All right, everyone seemed to be against her now, black had become white, a discarded wife was a bore and a nuisance and she had no experience of fighting for her rights, but it was different now; it was her children she was fighting for. And in the matter of children, mother nature was on her side against the big guns.

She got up, brushed the strawy grass off her skirt and went inside to ring the solicitor. The office was closed, of course, but she left a message on the answerphone saying she agreed with him that they had a fight on their hands, accepted the need for a barrister, was prepared to take Duncan to court if necessary and please could she come to see Mr Coffey as soon as possible. Then, pulling a face at the taste of it, she swallowed a glass of brandy and went upstairs to see to her mother.

Twenty-One

M r Hardcastle was a meticulous man. Within four days
Flora had received from him a detailed report of his
findings and proposals for a financial scheme to release funds
to maintain her mother's flat, which he would like to discuss
with her, as soon as was convenient. A very courteous covering letter thanked her for her hospitality and delicious tea and
suggested that in return he might, on his next visit, have the
pleasure of taking her out to lunch.

"He fancies you, Mum," Liz said, on reading the letter.

"Don't be silly. He's only being polite."

"He looks the sort who'd take you somewhere really posh."

"I can't leave Gran. He can have lunch here with us."

"Of course you must go. It'll do you good. I'll come back a
bit early from work and give Gran her lunch. Speaking of
work, it's time I was off."

She kissed her mother and ran out of the kitchen, thinking
that she was really enjoying this rôle reversal, this mothering
of her own mother.

She thought this again the following week, as she stood at
the front door and watched Mr Hardcastle lead her mother
out to his car and open the passenger door for her. Her
mother, she noticed approvingly, got in more elegantly than
most women manage to do. In fact her mother, she thought,
looked pretty good, given that she was forty-six. The day was
warm and she was wearing a favourite summer dress, lavender
and white, with a fitted bodice and full skirt. She wasn't all
bulgy and baggy like some people's mothers and she didn't

overdo the make-up, thank goodness, nor did her hair have that lacquered, straight-from-under-the dryer look that makes middle-aged coiffures so boring. Her mother's hair looked as if it had actually grown the way it was. True, she did have a few lines on her face, but that was only because she did a lot of thinking and, until recently, quite a lot of laughing too. And she had good legs.

Mr Hardcastle drove fast, evidently familiar with these narrow winding roads. As she relaxed in the passenger seat, Flora realised that for the past few months she had always either driven herself or been a somewhat nervous passenger with one of her inexperienced children at the wheel. She could sit back now, as she had always done with Duncan, and enjoy the passing countryside. The roadside banks were bright with midsummer flowers, with swathes of white cow parsley, interspersed with yellow yarrow and tall foxgloves, all the simple, easily recognisable flowers familiar from childhood.

"I hope you will like the The Horse and Groom," Mr Hardcastle began. "Everything there is unpretentious but of excellent quality, Mrs Maltby."

"Oh, please do call me Flora, surnames are so formal."

"Thank you, though there is nothing reprehensible about formality," he said, glancing at her with a little smile of mock reproof. "My name is Martin."

If he goes on like this, the lunch will be quite a strain, Flora thought, not sure how much was affectation and how much was just the way he really was.

They didn't talk much; he concentrated on his fast driving, while she enjoyed watching the hedgerows go by, glancing now and then at the long, pale fingers on the steering wheel.

The Horse and Groom was a mellow brick building lying well back from the road. It had been extended, but the alteration had been so perfectly done that it was impossible to tell where the old building ended and the new began. Tables were laid outside, shaded by big orange umbrellas, surrounded by lawns and flowerbeds.

"I have of course booked a table inside," Martin Hardcastle said. "Nothing could be more disagreeable than eating out of doors in the heat, don't you agree?"

Actually she'd thought that the tables with their bright umbrellas had a very continental, inviting look, but she agreed politely and followed him inside.

Once indoors, following him across the stone-flagged floor of the inn to a quiet table by a north-facing window, looking out over a cool and secluded little garden, she realised how right he had been.

"I can recommend their pâté," he told her. "I believe it has been made for them for many years by a farmer's wife in the village. Their claret matches it very nicely."

And so it was with everything on the menu.

"You seem to know this inn particularly well?" Flora remarked when the ordering was at last finished, the wine poured.

"My work compels me to travel and to eat out a great deal so I have, of necessity, become familiar with hotels and inns and have over the years selected those which appeal to me most. I detest large hotels which are overpriced and pretentious and tend to contain too many people doing work similar to my own."

"So you don't like to talk shop with them?"

He looked at her, aghast.

"Indeed not. I deplore all such talk. I find my work quite loathsome. It has to be done and there's an end to it."

It was such an unexpected remark that at first she thought she must have misheard him.

"But you're so good at what you do," she objected, buttering her toast, "so quick to understand. I mean I've seen that in the way you've dealt with my mother's affairs and all the plans you explained to me this morning."

"If something has to be done, it must be well done," he told

her, but at the same time smiled at her, a secret, even conspiratorial little smile which somehow illuminated his face,
revealing a different, warmer person. Perhaps he just put on
this punctilious persona as part of the disguise, like the formal
clothes, the furled umbrella, which he adopted for the work he
said he found so uncongenial.

"It offends me, you see," he was saying, "to find that a
client has capital withering away in building societies or
slumbering in gilts. It is my duty to make it work efficiently
for them."

"And for yourself?" she asked, emboldened by claret.

He smiled.

"Away from work," he said, "I prefer to put my mind to my
books and my garden. These are the true riches."

They were quiet for a while concentrating on locally produced pheasant and vegetables picked that morning, he assured her, from the kitchen garden beyond that high wall just
visible through their window.

"It seems a pity," she said at last, "that you couldn't have
chosen to do something you *did* enjoy."

"I tried."

"I'm sorry – I shouldn't . . ." she began, embarrassed.

"No, please, the question was justified by what I have said,"
he reassured her, briefly touching her hand. "I came of a land-
owning family and wanted to farm. My attempt at it, under-
capitalised and inexperienced as I was, failed. Dismally. I was
a bad farmer. Somewhere along the road I found I had a way
with figures. It is some kind of knack, a way of looking at
things, nothing more."

"It's a knack most of us don't have, alas." She hesitated and
then asked, "How did you get to know my mother? She never
told me, you know. So if it's confidential—"

"By no means. I was working in the trustee department of
an insurance firm handling all the private clients in the home
counties. Your mother's solicitor gave her a list of firms that
might help to handle her affairs and she chose ourselves. It was

by chance that I was given the honour of taking care of her. When she felt she was beginning to become occasionally confused she arranged, with her solicitor, that I should have power of attorney as and when it became necessary."

"How strange that we knew nothing of this."

"I should have preferred it otherwise, but Mrs Sutton had strong views. She felt that such matters are better dealt with outside the family. It is a great joy to me – and I am sure a benefit to her – that you and I are now in touch, though I do of course regret the circumstances which have brought this about."

He paused and glanced at her in a way which indicated that this was the only reference he would make to Duncan's departure.

"I do recommend the strawberries," he went on. "They are little wild ones which grow on the banks around the grounds. They are truly delicious, quite unlike the overlarge and taste-less variety grown for the modern market."

They were sweet and luscious and tasted like no other strawberries she had ever eaten.

When she told him, as they drove home, that it was the best meal she'd had in years, she was not exaggerating.

"I hope it will not be the only one we shall enjoy together," he told her, as he took her hand in farewell.

She watched the car disappear down the drive and stood for a moment enjoying the sense of euphoria that the day had bestowed. Of course, she told herself, it's the effect of the claret and the muscatel and of that final fine cognac; abstemious himself, Martin Hardcastle had plied her with so many good things. And the spoiling, of course, and the sunshine had added to it. And the fascination of listening to this compli-cated man. How odd he was, how full of contradictions. He seemed genuinely to despise the money he was so good at managing. And the thought of his ever being a farmer – with those long fingers, pale and tapering! No wonder it hadn't worked. She knew she wouldn't have found him so intriguing if Duncan had still been there. "Odd bloke, that," Duncan would have said and that would have been that.

She walked round to the back of the house where Liz and Nick were starting to decorate.

"How did it go, Mum?" Liz asked, putting down the block of wood covered in sandpaper with which she'd been rubbing the back door.

"It was lovely, I was utterly spoiled."

"You look gorgeous," Liz said, kissing her on the nose. "It's too hot for a proper hug. I reckon it did you a lot of good being taken out and you should do it more often. Take your mind off things."

"And how have you got on?"

"Well, we're short of sandpaper so Nick's just gone to the DIY to get some more. Gran's asleep in the hammock. I've fed all of us and I'm sorry about the mess in the kitchen."

"I haven't been in there yet."

"You'll be pretty appalled. But I thought we ought to get on outside while the weather holds."

"Don't worry, darling. I'll soon get it tidied up."

Liz had not exaggerated; the kitchen table and all working surfaces were strewn with dirty dishes. Half-filled saucepans, some with blackened vegetables still floating in them, occupied the sink. Something had boiled over and burnt on the cooker. It was a far cry from home-made pâté and wild strawberries.

Back to reality, she thought as she went upstairs to change. As she peeled off the lavender dress she seemed to shed with it all the euphoria of the afternoon. She had been a different person then, confident, admired, cherished, as she had once been by Duncan.

Tears filled her eyes as she put on an old cotton dress and with it assumed again all the worries and fears that had beset her since he left. She still feared she might lose the house. And could she really expect Milly to look after her mother when she started work in October? If her mother got worse she'd need professional, expensive care. And she was worried about the legal situation too. Mr Coffey had contacted a barrister whom she desperately wanted to meet but Mr Coffey said she mustn't do so until they all met together for the final settlement. She didn't want to put the ending of her marriage into the hands of a stranger who knew nothing of her or her family. She needed to know people who worked for her, needed them to be friends.

As always when she began to worry, the pain of Duncan's duplicity and the treachery of his parents struck her anew and the weight of it all seemed literally to press on her shoulders, so that she felt forced to sit down on the bed. The worst part, she thought, as she sat, head in hands, was what was happening to the children. All their lives they'd come first and now Duncan had put them nowhere.

She tried to tell herself that perhaps it had brought out strengths in them that they wouldn't otherwise have had, reminded herself of the number of times she'd thought recently how wonderfully they had behaved, how loyally, how lovingly. But it didn't work. *They shouldn't have to* was all she could think now.

Then, wearily, she got off the bed, told herself it was just part of the way things were now; all of them, Nick, Liz and herself were unsettled, sometimes confident, sometimes inexplicably cast down. She didn't seem to be in charge of her emotions nowadays. She coped with big problems that she'd had time to think about, then some small unexpected thing upset her. As it is for the bereaved, she thought, so it is for me. This afternoon was a happy interlude, a little peak in the ups and downs of life as it now is so I must expect to fall into a trough afterwards. Thus resolved she went downstairs to face the horrors of the kitchen.

Twenty-Two

The air was fresh with a touch of early autumn as Flora walked along the Embankment from the tube station. She'd had quite a battle with Mr Coffey to be allowed to do what she planned at this meeting, namely put the barrister in the picture, get him to see what kind of family she had.

"It really isn't necessary, Mrs Maltby," he had said to her, looking more worried now about this possible breach of etiquette than he had done about what seemed to her more serious matters on her previous visits. "I have collated all the available financial information; Mr Talbot will be concerned with that and advising us about the course we should take when we meet the other side next week."

"I do understand that, but it matters to me that he should know about my family, know that I'm not a grasping person, I don't want much for myself – I shall be getting a job anyway – but I must have enough to keep the home going and look after Liz and Nick. I simply want him to know something about us. It's our future we're entrusting to him. I just don't want to entrust it to a stranger."

In the end he had given in, rather to her surprise, so here she was walking along the Embankment with a bagful of family photographs and school reports. All right, it might not be the conventional thing to do, but it was her family that she wanted him to fight for, so the more he knew about them the better.

There was room for very few cars along the narrow street, but outside his Chambers was a tiny parking lot with his name on it. It might just have accommodated a mini: his azure blue Rolls Royce overlapped all the white lines.

She stood looking at it, suddenly taken aback by the grandeur of it. Am I helping to pay for *that*? she wondered. Have I really raided my building society savings account, which Duncan might or might not reimburse, to help maintain his Rolls Royce? I who compare the prices of packets of butter in the supermarket? What's happened to me? And Nick, who watched the water meter going round, what would he have to say of this vast expenditure?

Then she saw them: on the back seat of the Rolls lay a cot blanket, a rag doll, an assortment of squashed smartie tubes, some pieces of jigsaw and a small packet of raisins. So he was a family man and to his children this was just any old car. He would understand. Suddenly more confident, she walked inside and presented herself to a secretary who led her upstairs to a small room where Mr Talbot awaited her.

"Mr Coffey will be here shortly," he said as they shook hands. "He has been delayed, so we have a little time to ourselves."

He was younger than she'd expected, even though she'd seen the evidence of little children in his car. He had very bright brown eyes and an air of singular alertness. He was fresh-complexioned and his features were very clear cut, the sort people describe as chiselled. A nice sort of face to see on the pillow beside you when you wake up in the morning, she thought, and hoped he had a nice wife.

He listened intensely in a way few people do, as if every word mattered to him. She told him about Nick and how he was going to start his civil engineering course next month and about Liz and her university course starting at the same time. His interest in her children was genuine; she could tell by the questions he asked. She noticed that he was very well-informed about both their courses and seemed to know exactly how the new student support system worked.

He was delighted that she'd brought the family album.

"Nobody has ever done such a thing before," he told her as he turned pages, remarking on them from time to time. "Oh, I like that one. My youngest is just about that size now. They're not at all alike are they? Very unidentical twins. Is that what you say? Unidentical? Whatever has she got on her head? Oh, the guinea pig, is it? I didn't recognize what it was from its backside. She's trusting. You can't potty train guinea pigs, can you? At least we've never managed it."

He perused the last school reports. She noticed that he read very fast, but nothing escaped his eye.

"It looks as if they've chosen just the right courses for their particular gifts," he said. "What are they doing now? Travelling?"

"No, they were going to. Nick was going backpacking in India and Liz was going to France, but when this happened—"

"You mean your husband leaving you?"

"Yes, that's right. I'm sorry it's still not easy to say. Well, then they both decided not to go away. They wanted to be with me and they wanted to earn money, so they've found themselves jobs."

He looked thoughtful and was about to say something when they were interrupted by the arrival of Mr Coffey. After greeting them both he settled himself, Flora noticed, a little apart from the two of them, an observer rather than a participator, as the barrister talked to her.

Mr Talbot asked her a few questions about her house and garden, about the children's needs, noted a few figures, swiftly prodded a calculator and then told her how much he thought she should reasonably be able to manage on in a year and how much would be required to produce that sum.

She looked at him in amazement; it was almost exactly the figure she herself had reached after days and days of calculations. Only fifty pounds a year difference between the two and he'd reached it in minutes.

"In my view he can easily afford this sum," he said, addressing them both. "From the information that you," glancing at the solicitor, "have collated, we know his salary, have an approximate idea of his new partner's salary and know there is a strong probability that he has recently inherited a considerable sum which would previously have been shared with his wife and children."

"And if he goes on offering us fifty pounds a week?" Flora asked.

"Oh, if he doesn't talk sense, we'll take him to court," Mr Talbot assured her.

Her face fell; this was the outcome she most dreaded.

"But I rather think he will talk sense," he added, smiling as he shook her hand.

"Until Tuesday then."

By Tuesday the weather had reverted to summer, all taint of autumn forgotten. Later they said it was the hottest September day on record. And late September at that.

The meeting was to be held in the offices of Duncan's solicitor, a concession which Mr Talbot thought it wise to make. Duncan, his solicitor and barrister were put into one room, herself and her two lawyers in another. For a moment they were all together in the entrance hall and she saw that Duncan was being introduced to his barrister by his solicitor. She also saw that whereas she had dressed up for the occasion, he had donned an old anorak, which, Mr Talbot explained afterwards, was a ploy quite often employed by husbands wanting to keep the alimony down. Poor Duncan, she thought; it would take more than an old anorak to fool my Mr Talbot.

She wanted to talk to him, but Duncan only nodded briefly and after that avoided her eye and was obviously relieved when the two parties went their divided ways. The procedure had been explained to her, but it still seemed odd. It was a very strange way to behave, she thought, as she stayed alone in her room, the lawyers going off to negotiate with Duncan's lawyers, coming back to report progress, seeking more instructions, going back again. So strange that she could hardly believe it was actually happening.

Duncan and I used to talk everything over, she thought, important or trivial: schools, insurance policies, how much we could afford to spend on holidays, what vegetables to plant, whether to get a new washing machine or spend the money on mending the roof and hope the old machine would last another twelve months. Everything and anything we talked about and now strangers have to come and carry messages between us as if we were two warring camps.

We are two warring camps.

The three of them had lunch together in a nearby pub. The others, Mr Coffey reported, were having sandwiches sent up.

"Sign of nerves," he commented. "They daren't leave the fortress."

They laughed a lot over the meal, not that she could eat much; it was too hot. She wondered how Liz and Nick were surviving as they finished painting the south-facing windows of the house.

"You're not nervous?" Mr Talbot asked.

"No," she shook her head. "Just not hungry."

"Because it's going well. I don't think your husband briefed his man as well as you did yours."

"Poor Duncan."

She spoke instinctively, without thinking how ironic it was. For so many years she had thought of him as deserving her support, her compassion. It was hard to change that instinct in a matter of months.

Both men looked at her in surprise.

"You needn't worry," Mr Talbot assured her. "We know what resources he has. He can part with the sum we requested without noticing any difference to his way of life. No need to feel sorry for him."

"It wasn't that. I'm just sorry he didn't go about it more sensibly. It was the sort of thing I used to help him with."

So, still only half-believing that all this was actually happening, she made her way back to Duncan's solicitor's office for the afternoon's negotiations. Somewhere in this building, in another room, she reflected, Duncan too will be sitting alone, as I am, while the lawyers talk.

Thinking of his lonely vigil made her forget for a moment that they were on different sides. She had a brief sense of fellow feeling with him, as if the division was really between them, two ordinary mortals who had got themselves into an extraordinary mess, and the four lawyers for whom such messes were simply a part of the daily round, who lived in a different world and sometimes spoke a different language.

Mr Talbot and the other barrister must know each other, she realised, just as the two solicitors did. Did they too have lunch together, did they shake their heads over their clients' weaknesses and foibles or just calculate their fees and decide they could afford another bottle of claret?

Twenty-Three

" **S** o that's it," Liz said, taking a final dab with the paint brush at the woodwork round the study window. "Thank God. I don't think I could have gone on much longer in this heat."

"A pity Mum wouldn't let us do the bedroom windows," Nick said glancing upwards.

"No, she was right, Nick. Swaying around on ladders at that height isn't a job for the unskilled."

"We're not unskilled any more," her brother objected indignantly. "We've painted a whole house."

"That'll look great on your CV," she told him, as they gathered up brushes, pots of paint and handfuls of dirty newspaper and began taking it all round to the toolshed.

They made their way slowly across the lawn, all movement dulled by the intense heat. The grass was so dry that it rustled as they walked.

"What's the temperature on the outdoor thermometer, Nick?"

He stopped and squinnied at the thermometer that hung in the shade at the back of the house.

"Nearly eighty-nine. And that's in the shade. I can't think what it was in the sun."

"Melting point, whatever that is," she told him as they went into the toolshed, which even in this heat had a damp, earthy smell. "Where's the white spirit gone?"

He handed it to her and they stood at the paint-splashed work bench cleaning brushes, squashing them down into jam jars of paint remover, and then wiping them on rags which had once been clothes.

"I recognise this one," Nick said suddenly. "A bit of Dad's pyjamas."

"Chuck it out when you've finished," his sister told him. "Hack it up first though," she added, nodding towards some garden shears that were hanging on the wall.

"You feel pretty savage about him still, don't you?"

"Yes, I bloody well do. When I think of those moralising lectures he used to give me. Nothing I ever did was one tenth as bad as what he's done."

She pressed the lid down on half a can of paint and began banging it home with a hammer.

"Don't you feel savage about him too?" she asked, giving the lid a final ferocious whack.

He nodded. "I don't think Mum does, though. And watch what you're doing, Liz. We might want to get that lid off again one day."

"It's odd really about Mum," Liz said, abandoning her onslaught on the paint tin. "I mean it's much worse for her than it is for us and yet she doesn't seem awfully bitter. In her shoes I'd find out where he was and kill him."

"No point, you'd only get gaoled for life."

"With remission, only ten years. It would be worth it," Liz told him, beginning to rub her hands with a rag soaked in white spirit.

"I hope she's getting on all right at that meeting. She seemed so hopeful. It would be awful if it was another disappointment."

"Yes. She looked really shattered after Dad's parents behaved like they did. I wouldn't mind having a go at them either. I just don't know how they could—"

"They're old, Liz—"

"Yes, but they're not batty, like Gran."

"And he *is* their son."

"They're welcome to him as far as I'm concerned."

"You don't say things like that to Mum, do you?"
She shook her head.
"No, only to you, Nick. You're my safety valve."
She stretched up and gave him a quick kiss on the cheek.
Then she handed him the rag and added, "Do clean your
hands or you'll get paint on to everything."
"Sometimes," he said, "you talk more like my mother than
my twin. Except," he added, "that Mum never talks like that."
"I hate to think of leaving her alone when we both go away
in October, Nick. It's only a week away now."
"We've got to go. She'd have a fit if we said we wouldn't."
"I know.
"She'll be all right, Liz, and we'll ring a lot and get home
when we can. Cheer up. I've just thought of something. You
remember when we were doing the utility we saw those two big
bottles of cider?"
"Yes."
"Do you think Mum would mind if we took them out to
celebrate finishing the house?"
"Of course she wouldn't mind. We bloody well deserve it."
"I'll put them in the fridge while we wash," Nick told her as
they left the toolshed and walked across the yard and into the
house.
"Do you want anything to eat with it? We haven't eaten all
day."
"No, it's too hot. Just lovely cool cider, that's all I need."
"Me too. God, shall I be glad to take off this paint dress."
She had worn the same dress for painting every day. It was
now stiff with emulsion paint, undercoat and gloss.
"I'm going to bin it, or maybe ceremoniously commit it to
the bonfire. Plus two bath caps. I don't know how you kept so
clean, apart from your hands."
"I'm just better at painting," he told her. "Come on, let's get
going."
"I'm going to have a quick bath."
"Must you? It takes more water than a shower."

"I said bath, Nick, because you've got this arrangement for saving water and it doesn't work in the shower."

"I hadn't thought of that. Maybe I could fix something—"

"Shut up, it's bad enough to have that hose pipe cluttering up the bath and dripping through the window."

So squabbling fitfully they made their way upstairs.

"Two hours to go before Mum gets back from London," Liz said after they'd washed. "Maybe three. And I've put the supper ready and Gran's asleep so I reckon we can relax and get drunk on cider."

"I don't think," Nick said as he carried the tray down the garden, "that cider's particularly alcoholic, is it? Let's drink it here, under the apple tree."

"Oh, yes it is. It's jolly alcoholic. And this was some especially strong stuff the parents brought back from Devon last year. Can't think why it's been sitting around unopened for so long."

"Soon put that right," Nick said, opening a bottle and pouring out the cider.

"Oh, it looks good. My, but it *is* good. Here's to you."

"And to you, Liz. To both of us."

They took deep gulps of the cold, tawny liquid, then sighed with satisfaction.

"Let's drink a toast to painters everywhere," Nick suggested.

Again they drank deeply.

After toiling in the heat, the cider seemed to slide down their dry throats, nectar-like and cooling.

"Yummy, it's better than champagne, this stuff."

"Let's drink a toast to Mum."

They both raised their glasses and drank to their mother.

"I say," Liz said suddenly. "Since we've drunk Mum's health, let's drink a toast of *ill* health to Fiona from Publicity."

"Wouldn't that be rather awful?"

"Nothing terminal." She told him. "Just undignified."

She stood up.

174

"To Fiona of Publicity. A solemn toast. May she get incurable dandruff."

So they both stood and drank the toast, though with some difficulty because they were laughing so much. Slowly they sank back on to the ground, tears of mirth starting from their eyes.

"I propose another toast," Nick said, raising his glass but not standing up.

Liz managed to struggle to her feet.

"Here's to Fiona, may she get veruccas," Nick proposed, speaking very slowly and solemnly and then collapsing into giggles, while Liz drank and laughed, holding on to the tree for support.

"Oh, this laughing really hurts," she said, sliding down to sit again on the grass under the apple tree.

Nick poured the last of the cider into her glass.

"It's amazing how quickly it's all gone," Liz said, looking in exaggerated surprise at the empty bottle.

"I'd better go and get the other one."

"Who'd have thought we'd have drunk it so quickly?" Liz pondered, shaking her head.

She watched as her brother made his way up to the house. He wasn't walking quite straight, she thought. Or maybe she wasn't seeing quite straight.

She had her toast ready when he got back.

"Here's to Fiona from Publicity. May she get haem— haem— haem—" She couldn't get the word out for laughing. "Piles!" she managed to shriek at last.

It struck them as being so terribly funny that they couldn't manage to drink at first. Finally they were calm enough to down the cider in great mouthfuls.

"We should get out of the sun," Nick said. "Look we're not in the shade any more. It's moved round."

"What a mean trick."

Carefully holding their glasses while Nick held the bottle, Liz shuffled round the tree. He followed.

"Sbetter," he said, leaning against the tree, eyes closed. "Syour turn. For a toasht."

"Here's to Fiona from Publishity," he proposed, speaking very slowly and deliberately. "May she get a big boil on her bottom."

"That's bashic but very good," Liz told him, as they both curled up with laughter.

"There's only enough for one more," he told her tragically.

"Then I propose Here's to Fiona from Publishity and may she get thrush," Liz intoned.

"Thrush? Thatsh a little bird. Too good for Fiona from Publishity. Try again, Liz."

"Not this thrush. This thrush is very ticklish and nashty. I know."

"Whatshit like? Whershit tickle?"

"On her pu—, pu—" Laughter prevented her getting the word out.

"On her poo? Like the shpaniel did on the lawn?"

They were both laughing helplessly now, rolling on the dry and rustling grass.

"No. On her pudenda," Liz managed to enunciate at last.

"Whatsh her pud— whateveryousaid."

"Ignorant boy. It's what Milly callsh her—" Laughter got in the way again. "What Milly callsh her Naughty Bits," she managed to burst out at last.

Flora parked the car carefully in the shady side of the garage and went indoors. It was very quiet; no sign of Nick and Liz who were usually all agog as they waited for her to come back from these legal sessions.

Perhaps they were still painting, she thought, as she went out again and walked round the front of the house. It looked wonderful, the white paint gleaming, everything cleared away, no splashes on the windows. They'd made a very professional job of it all.

How they'd grown up in these past few months, how they'd

worked uncomplainingly at their jobs and at helping her in the house. She must give them a treat before they left. Yes, she'd take them to dinner at Tilley's. She could afford it now and they deserved something really special.

At least Nick hadn't had to cut the grass this past dry month, she thought as she walked across the parched lawn and down to the orchard. Then she saw them, the pair of them sprawled under the apple tree, glasses and two large empty cider bottles alongside, fast asleep.

She stood looking down at them for a moment, wondering whether to wake them, but they seemed so peaceful, both smiling as they slept, that she decided that the good news could keep until later.

Twenty-Four

"About next Thursday," Liz said, helping herself to another croissant, "I don't think we should both leave on the same day."

The two of them were sitting over a late breakfast, the newspapers strewn across the kitchen table.

"Why not?" Nick said, looking up from the sports pages.

"Well, think of poor Mum, being left all on her own so suddenly. I think we should go in dribs and drabs."

"Or tits and farts, as Gran said the other day."

"She didn't!"

"Yes, she told me I ought to do things straightalong and I was always doing things in tits and farts."

"It's weird, isn't it? I mean the way she sometimes talks sense but with the words all knotted up. She's pretty lucid at the moment. Falling out of the hammock last week really seemed to do her a power of good."

"Yes, I've noticed too. I even explained to her how to tip spare water into her lavatory cistern and she understood, I know she did."

"Oh, Nick, must you really still bang on about the water meter? Now Mum's got the house and enough money to run it, does it matter?"

"Yes, she's got enough, but only just. And anyway I like economising. I think it's healthy. *And* it's good for the environment."

He hesitated, then went on, "Liz, you don't think Mum will go, well, a bit peculiar, like Gran, do you?"

Liz shook her head, "No. It isn't hereditary, Mum said."

"Well, she would say that, wouldn't she? She wouldn't want us worrying."

"True. But the fact is that they don't really know what's wrong with Gran. They thought about Alzheimer's but apparently she doesn't have all the right symptoms."

"I read about that the other day. It said you can't tell for sure until they're dead. When Gran dies they'll be able to take her brain out and find out what was wrong with her."

"Much good that'll do! Then they thought it was some kind of dementia with a long name I can't remember. But I agree with Mum that it doesn't really matter what it's called since no diagnosis helps to get a cure. Shove the marmalade over, will you?"

"Well, what about Thursday?" he asked, passing her the jar.

"No, the other one. I like the sort Mum makes with great chunks of orange peel in it."

He passed her the other jar.

"I could wait until Friday morning," she suggested piling the lumpy marmalade on to the croissant.

"Right. I'll go on Thursday afternoon and you go on Friday."

"It's going to be awful for her, you know."

"I dunno, she might enjoy a bit of peace. It would make a change for her."

"Come off it, Nick! Just think of being all on her own here, no Dad, no us, just poor old Gran and probably quite a lot of Milly Chatterton."

"Maybe that Hardcastle chap will take her out some more. She's been out to lunch with him twice now."

He paused, then added anxiously, "You don't think she'll marry him, do you?"

Liz shook her head.

"Absolutely not."

Then, because she'd never quite forgiven Martin Hardcastle for the failure of her tea party plot, she added, "You've only got to look at him to see he's anally retentive."

"What's that mean?"

"Oh, you *know*," Liz said and then, not being sure herself, went on quickly, "but it's nice for her to be taken out now and then. Good for her morale. And thank goodness, she's got the job to go to. But it'll still mean she's on her own a lot and weekends will drag. I could kill that bloody father of ours."

"Sh, she doesn't like us to say such things."

"You can talk! You were the one that hit him."

Nick couldn't think of any reply, so handed her another croissant instead and they sat peacefully together, drinking coffee, absent-mindedly spreading butter and marmalade on rolls and croissants, while they read the paper, now and then handing pages of it to each other across the table.

There was no sound in the kitchen apart from the occasional rustling of newsprint and the scraping of knife on bread. The pendulum clock continued its loud ticking, but since it had been a background noise for as long as they could remember, they were unaware of it.

"Do you know what I think?" Liz asked suddenly.

"What?"

"It'll be jolly odd going to college. I mean everyone there will be normal."

He nodded.

"I've been thinking that. We've got used to this, haven't we? A dad that's gone off and a mad gran. Ordinary people are going to seem quite weird."

"Or innocent?"

"Mm."

They sat thinking about it, not talking. After a while Liz said, "But we don't know, do we? I mean it could be that the others have weird families too."

"Mad grans?"

She shrugged.

"Maybe. Maybe alcoholic mums, violent dads, delinquent siblings, any old thing. And they'll be thinking how normal we are and we'll be thinking how normal they are and really nobody's normal."

"Speak for yourself," Flora said, coming into the kitchen. "How are the hangovers this morning?"

"We didn't have hangovers," Nick told her indignantly. "And if we did it was because there was something odd about that cider."

"Well, let's just say you both look a lot better this morning than you did yesterday. Any coffee left in that pot?"

Liz peered into the jug.

"I'll warm it up," she said.

"And it was really clever of you to celebrate before you even knew about the outcome of the meeting," Flora went on.

"Actually it was finishing painting the house that we were celebrating," Nick told her. "But it's great about the settlement, Mum. We're quite proud of you, actually, aren't we, Liz?"

"Oh," Flora began, but couldn't go on. It was she who was proud of them and she didn't deserve this unexpected praise. That and the relief of not having to worry any more about being penniless was suddenly too much to bear. She stood, looking at them, shaking her head, unable to speak.

Liz came and put her arms around her.

"Why don't you go and sit outside, Mum," she said gently, "while it's still sunny? I'll bring you some coffee out, then Nick and I'll clear up the mess in here."

Flora nodded, still unable to speak; she leant against her daughter for a moment, aware of being mothered by her and grateful for it.

How we have looked after each other, she thought as she sat on the patio, coffee and paper on the table alongside, slowly relaxing and beginning to enjoy the autumn sunshine. She could remember now with tranquillity how she had sat here nearly six months ago, alongside Duncan, everything so normal, no hint that it would be their last weekend together.

It seemed like a different life; she sighed as she remembered it, but there was no anguish now; the wound was healing, the days of being able to think of nothing except longing for him to be back were over, as were the ceaseless arguments she had had with herself about why it had all happened, tormenting herself with fruitless speculation. She still had bad moments and knew there would be more of them but that the troughs, when they came, would be shallower and the gaps between them wider.

What filled her with dread now, she had to acknowledge to herself, was the thought of Liz and Nick going away, of the great emptiness they would leave behind. She could hear them through the open kitchen window. How silent it would be when they left! But there it is, she told herself, it is right that they should go and I shall just try not to think about it and make the most of having them alone with me for a couple of days after mother goes away for her week's respite. And I was lucky to be able to a get a table for Tuesday at Tilley's when they're always so booked up. So I shall count my blessings, relax for a while, let them see how much I appreciate their care.

Thus resolved, she lay back, newspaper ignored as she listened to the squawking of the birds as they fought over the breakfast crumbs on the lawn and to the chattering of her children as they laughed and argued over the washing up.

Twenty-Five

W hen they founded the establishment that bore their name, Francis and Emmanuella Tilley aimed at combining in it the relaxed atmosphere of a private dinner party with the service of a restaurant. This, by careful attention to every detail, they largely succeeded in doing.

Their guests came only by appointment and were expected to arrive by eight o'clock. They were welcomed, their coats taken away and the doors locked behind them, so that there would be no disruption caused by new arrivals pushing past tables, bringing in gusts of the outside world. Private at their individual tables though the diners were, they nonetheless felt like house guests. The room was not very large and folding doors partially divided the space into two, each the size of a country house dining room.

There were no menus on the table, no rush to make choices. Leisurely girls in long dresses brought round hors d'oeuvres, while others offered baskets of a myriad varieties of bread of every colour and shape. After a while silver tureens of soup were placed on the table.

"Watch it," Liz warned as Nick ladled himself out a third helping. "According to Mum there are at least five more courses to come."

"Golly, what a place," her brother exclaimed, momentarily laying down his spoon.

"It's all right, darling," Flora assured him, "there's plenty of time. Look, it says, 'Carriages at 11.30.' The idea is that people come here to make an evening of it."

"It's great, Mum. Easily the best place we've ever been to."

"Well, you both deserve a treat. And, yes, it *is* different."

"Have you been here often then?"

"About two or three times, I suppose. Your father occasionally brought business people here."

She regretted the remark; mention of Duncan always caused constraint. They were silent as the soup plates and tureen were removed, all of them aware that this was the first time they'd been out for a family meal like this without him.

"It seems odd, not having a menu," Liz said, to break the silence.

"They come and tell you what's on offer, then they show you, so you can see if you like the look of it. Look, here they come."

As she spoke, the girls appeared to show them the fish course and the vegetarian alternative.

Flora chose the saumon en papillotte, Liz the vegetarian terrine and Nick looked from one to the other, said he couldn't decide and really liked them both.

"That can be arranged," the girl said. They were trained to be indulgent.

"Nick, you can't!" his sister told him. "The meal hasn't really started yet."

"Maybe you're right. I'll have the fish, please."

It was a warm evening. Later, as they were being served their palette-cleansing sorbets, the manager set going the big old-fashioned fan in the centre of the ceiling and pushed the partition between the two ends of the dining room further back to allow more circulation of air.

It was then that Flora saw them: the people sitting at the corner table which had been out of her line of vision before. There was something familiar about the figure sitting with his back to her, but at that distance it was hard to be certain; it was just something about the set of the broad shoulders, the greying hair, curling up at the back, thinning on top. Then he turned and in semi-profile there was no mistaking him. Undoubtedly Duncan.

"What is it, Mum?"

"Nothing, darling."

Blessedly they had their backs to him.

"Look, the girls are coming back for the orders for the next course," she said.

Boeuf à l'orange, roast pork, lamb chops with apricots, Aylesbury duckling, chicken Maryland, vegetarian goulash were brought round on salvers to be examined and chosen.

"I'll have duckling," Liz said.

"I thought you were a vegetarian?"

"Only for the first course, Nick."

"But you said—"

"Consistency is the last resort of feeble minds," she told him.

Flora only half-listened, smiling absently, her mind on the table on the other side of the partition. Opposite him was a young woman, blonde, poised, undoubtedly Fiona. But this wasn't a romantic *dîner à deux*. Two other men were there; one was young, like Fiona, the other nearer Duncan's age. No, this was business entertaining. She had once told Duncan that she thought the term a misnomer; they didn't seem to do much business and often it wasn't very entertaining.

"Courgettes, Mum?" Liz said, evidently not for the first time.

"Thank you, darling."

"And baby sweet corn. It'll go well with your chicken."

"Yes, of course. Thank you."

"Penny for them?"

"Sorry, darling. I was just wondering," she improvised, "How they manage to get these baby carrots at this time of the year. Mine only seem to keep that size in the spring."

"Perhaps they cut them like that out of big carrots? I expect I could do that for you if I tried."

She shook her head.

"No, you can tell they're young carrots. Besides they have such a sweet taste."

"You could plant them later," Nick put in. "Next year I could keep planting them through the summer then there'd always be young ones."

"Thank you, darling," Flora said, touched by this outburst of concern from a daughter who had no interest in cooking and a son who had none in gardening, other than grass cutting. These had always been purely parental concerns. She couldn't help wondering what Duncan would have thought of it; once they would have smiled together at such unexpected changes in their children.

She could see him more clearly now. He didn't seem to be saying very much. The young pair were doing most of the talking. At the end of the main course he and the older man got up and went upstairs together. Presumably to the loo. Duncan was fifty, the prostate not functioning quite as well as it once did. The younger pair continued their animated conversation.

Duncan looked tired, she thought, observing him surreptitiously as he returned. He was looking his age. She had never thought of him as much older than herself; six years is nothing. But now she noticed it. Probably the contrast with her, with his new – what? Partner. Presumably they'd marry. Perhaps have children.

"What is it, Mum?"

"Oh, nothing darling. I was just thinking how unusual that flower arrangement is on the stand. Anthurium lilies and strelitzias. Both rather unnatural flowers, not exactly graceful, but they look lovely arranged like that."

Determinedly she concentrated on her children, on the meal, on the wine, on anything but the people at that table beyond the partition. To think that she had even been imagining Nick and Liz having step-siblings! It was too awful to contemplate, yet why not? It could happen.

"Just look at the puddings," she said.

The girls in long dresses had lined up, eight or nine of them, each bearing a serving dish which they proceeded to carry from table to table, displaying their wares: summer pudding, shiny and purple, oozing juice, a pyramid of profiteroles dripping with chocolate, coffee gâteau smothered in cream, luscious oranges soaked in brandy, old-fashioned sherry trifle, bread and butter pudding, apple pie and custard.

Liz and Nick watched, wide-eyed, this procession as it passed.

Flora chose profiteroles because she never made them at home, Liz said she couldn't eat another thing and Nick said he fancied the lot.

"Make up your mind," his sister told him. "They're waiting."

"If I have the summer pudding, you can have the apple pie and give it to me."

"All right. Pig."

"He's got a big frame, Liz," Flora demurred.

"It'll be bigger still by tomorrow."

Certainly Duncan is looking drawn and not saying much, Flora observed, as she pushed profiteroles around her plate. The younger pair are doing most of the talking. The young man is clearly taken with Fiona. Does that worry Duncan, I wonder? Or perhaps he's pleased to have a partner other men envy? A wife to be proud of. Don't think like that, Flora. It does you no good.

The girls came round again with the puddings.

"Perhaps you would like to try a different one?" they invited. "At home you would probably do that at a dinner party, wouldn't you?"

"I'll try the profiteroles this time," Nick said. "You can have the gâteau, Liz, and give it to me."

"Four puddings, oh my God. You *can't*, Nick.

Flora left them arguing and went upstairs to the ladies.

It was a pretty room, softly lit, furnished with easy chairs, bedecked with flowers. She took her time washing, drying her hands on the little individual towels, soft and scented, that surrounded the basins, combing her hair, improving her make-up, giving herself time to compose herself. She must get used to this. Inevitably their paths would sometimes cross, she told herself. It was just that she wasn't ready for it yet; seeing him, so familiar, yet now so strange, had shocked her.

At least the children hadn't seen him and with a bit of care she could get them out of the restaurant first. If he saw them, he would hold his party back, she thought, trying to reassure herself as she closed the door behind her.

There was a wide half-landing on the turn of the shallow stairs. As she came down she found herself face to face with Duncan. They stood looking at each other, the two of them, suddenly alone with each other, out of sight of everyone else; above them was silence, below them the buzz of distant conversation. They seemed isolated, there on the landing.

Suddenly he reached out, touched her hand.

"I'm sorry," he said and went quickly on, up the stairs.

She stood for a while, nonplussed. It wasn't just the suddenness of it, nor the surprise at what had been said by Duncan, who had never been much of a one for apologising, but at her own reaction to it. For a moment it had seemed he might be saying it was all a mistake that he regretted, that he wanted to come back to her and the children. She had been dismayed at the idea. She didn't want him back. That was what had surprised and shocked her, she realised as she went slowly downstairs to rejoin the others.

Twenty-Six

"How you can eat anything after last night at Tilley's I just don't know," Liz remarked, sipping her black coffee.

"I've only had cornflakes and toast, nothing cooked," her brother protested indignantly. "And just one croissant so far," he added, reaching for another.

"It was a wonderful place."

"I expect it was jolly expensive."

"Well, it did her good too, to get out."

"Where is she?"

"Getting Gran ready to go into respite tomorrow. She's so patient with her, Nick. Gran spends for ever deciding what clothes she wants to take and then always changes her mind at the last moment."

"Liz, I never know when they talk about respite, who it's supposed to be respite *for* – her or Mum?"

"All of us, I suppose."

"And I suppose it's respite time for *them* when she comes back here."

Liz laughed.

"'Spose so," she agreed.

They were quiet for a while, then Nick said, "Of course, if she *did* get married again – I don't mean to the Hardcastle chap, but to anyone else. Maybe someone we don't even know—"

"Nick," Liz interrupted. "She won't get married again. Just think about it. Why should Mum remarry? She's forty-six and she's got us."

* * *

Gran always enjoyed going back to the home. She had a particular corner of the day room which she liked to occupy and in which she was now installed in her favourite chair by the window. Flora was unpacking her case in the bedroom, Liz staying by her grandmother. Nick had opted out. He had, he said vaguely, things to sort out before he could pack; Flora, knowing how ill at ease he felt at the respite home, connived at this excuse.

Gran was surveying the other residents and day visitors.

"The one over there," she told Liz in a very loud whisper, "is very well off. She has an air-conditioned pension."

"Index-linked, you mean, Gran?"

"That's what I said."

She looked around proprietorially.

"I like this house of mine," she told Liz. "Of course they're a funny lot staying, but it takes all sorts, like the liquorice."

An elderly woman, sweet-faced and sombrely clad, made her way over to them and held out her hand.

"Australia," she said with a welcoming smile and walked away.

"She only has the one word," Gran remembered. "But she can do anything with it. It's a waste really, all those words in the dictionary and half of them never used. The money could be better spent."

"Does she live here or just visit like you?"

"Yes. And if she dressed better she'd be a good-looking woman. I prefer to be gift-wrapped myself."

Nowadays she particularly favoured vivid green, shocking pink and electric blue. She stood out among the assembled company like some tropical bird among a hedgerow of dunnocks.

Liz looked around her, suddenly stuck for something to say. At home they chattered away, meandering from topic to topic according to Gran's inconsequential thought processes, as if the conversation was being steered by a drunken navigator. Surrounded by normality, it didn't matter, but here it was different, more frightening somehow and she found herself at a loss for words.

In another corner a young nurse was squatting on the floor with a group of old ladies playing a simple game in which they were each dealt a few large cards; when the nurse put one down they had to match it with one of their own. They watched eagerly, utterly absorbed for the moment and when they managed to put down a card their wrinkled old faces had all the triumphant delight of a four-year-old.

I played something like that when I was little, Liz thought, and I expect they did too. And now they're playing it again. So it's true about second childhood. But what happened to the person who lived for all the years in between?

At least they looked animated, not like the ones sitting round the walls in high-backed chairs, expressionless and almost motionless. Nearby, an old man sat so still he might have been dead, his eyes closed, his hands resting on two sticks, their pale yellow skin stretched to translucency so that the veins showed like tiny threads of bright blue between the sharp ridges of the bones.

She mustn't stare. Must think of something to say.

"You must be one of the youngest here, Gran," she said, randomly.

Her grandmother shook her head.

"No, dear," she said, her voice suddenly very loud in the silent room. "I am by no means the youngest here, but I do have the best figure."

A few heads turned and, Liz thought, looked at her grandmother with considerable dislike. But maybe she imagined it.

"The trouble with today," her grandmother went on, "is that people no longer wear corsets. Corsets kept people upright. Rectitude, it was called. Moral rectitude. It went out with the corsets so nobody is moral any more."

"But Gran," Liz said, knowing she shouldn't argue, but unable to stop herself. "Men didn't wear corsets, so why should *they* be less moral?"

191

"Lord Cardigan was the last general to lead his men into battle wearing corsets," Gran began to contradict, then she looked puzzled and said with considerably less certainty, "And I *think* that's why they named the balaclava hat after him."

"Here's Mum coming back," Liz remarked after the short silence that followed this remark. "Shall I get you some coffee, Gran?"

"Only if it's decontaminated. The other sort keeps me awake."

"I'll get it, Liz," Flora said. "You go off now. I'll stay a bit longer."

Trying not to look as relieved as she felt, she stooped to kiss her grandmother, who gave a knowing little smile.

"Little Miss Judas," she said.

Liz looked at her mother, horrified, but her mother just shook her head and the look on her face said, *Don't worry, she means nothing by it, she just got hooked on the idea of the kiss.* There was such comfort, such reassurance in that look that she gave her mother a sudden impulsive hug and then turned and almost fled across the room.

"Don't look so sad," one of the nurses said. "We don't all end up like this, you know. It's only a very small percentage of us and for the most part the patients here are happy in their own way."

She thanked her and as she turned felt someone touch her arm. It was the sweet-faced, sombrely clad old lady. She too was looking at Liz with compassion. "Australia," she said consolingly. "Australia."

Outside the home, she breathed deeply. She hadn't noticed, when she came, how fresh the air was, how sharp with the tang of autumn. But after the stuffy stillness of the day room, the outside world seemed vibrant with life, movement and colour. She stood, trying to understand why she felt so guilty; she was sorry for her grandmother, of course she was, and for all the other inmates but oh, the unquenchable relief of escaping from them and from all the mustiness of old age.

"Bliss was it in that dawn to be alive, but to be young was very Heaven," she quoted to herself as, leaving guilt behind, she set off briskly down the road longing to get home and start her packing in readiness for the new life which stretched before her and suddenly seemed as fresh, invigorating and inviting as this tangy autumn morning.

Twenty-Seven

They had gone. The house was unnaturally silent. In the kitchen even the ticking of the pendulum clock seemed deafening. She went upstairs, first to Liz's bedroom and then to Nick's, gazing at the stripped beds, the empty shelves, touching familiar objects left behind, unwanted at college.

Of course they must go, it's right that they go, right too that they go so enthusiastically, but oh the pain of it. Last time when they had left, Duncan and I heaved a sigh of relief and said how peaceful it was after the turmoil of departure; make the most of it, we said, because any moment now the telephone will ring and they'll be wanting us to send something they've forgotten. But now there is just this desolation, for I have fulfilled my rôle and there is no more need for me.

Nonsense, tomorrow I shall wash linen, tidy cupboards, bring my mother back from respite and a new life will start. It must. On Monday I shall travel up to town, establish myself in my new office, leaving mother in the safe keeping of Milly Chatterton.

After thus arguing with herself she granted herself five minutes of self-indulgent grief, burying her head in her daughter's pillow and sobbing with loneliness. Then she got up, said, "That's enough of self-pity," combed her hair and began putting things ready for the morrow.

Her mother played the gracious lady as she left the home, responding to the muted farewells of the other inmates as if

194

acknowledging the plaudits of the crowds. In the car, she gave a little wave in the direction of the empty windows and tried to remove her safety belt.

"I hate this thing," she said, tugging at it. "No good to man or beast. Or good red herring," she added.

She was distracted by a string of horses approaching down the road. Flora stopped to let them by.

"Isn't that a beautiful white horse, Mother?" Flora remarked as the last one passed.

"White horse? White horse?" her mother repeated, a faraway look in her eyes as if she was searching her faulty memory for some lost recollection. "That's where they fly kites and propose marriage," she said.

"Oh, do they?"

So that was it; he wanted his ashes scattered where he had asked her to marry him, where his Anita had accepted him, where blissfully his brief happiness had begun.

"Is that what your husband did, propose to you there?" she asked, a few minutes later.

Her mother shrugged.

"Oh, husbands," she said. "We can do without them."

She speaks more appropriately than she knows, Flora thought, except that she did without hers from choice and I from necessity.

Milly Chatterton arrived in good time on Monday morning.

"I hope you don't mind," she said, "but I've brought the Thomson's puppy I'm looking after, in case it gets lonely back home, and I've brought their goldfish too, not that it would get lonely but I thought Anita might like to watch it going round and round. She likes anything like that. And I've brought bagatelle too, because I enjoy that and she likes the noise it makes. And—"

"I've left everything ready for your lunch in the kitchen, Milly," Flora interrupted. "I've made some soup which just needs warming and there's cold meat and salad and I thought you might like a baked potato with it and—"

"Don't you worry," Milly told her. "I'm ever so good at poking round other people's cupboards. I'll find everything we need, so you just go off and enjoy yourself."

"This is my office number if you need to ring. Don't hesitate if you have any worries."

"Oh, everything will be fine, don't you worry. We'll have a great time. How about a cup of coffee, Anita? I know I could do with one. And then we'll have a stroll in the garden, shall we, and a game or two back here? I've put the puppy's lead round the table leg so he doesn't trip you up and the goldfish doesn't like direct sunlight so I'll just pop it in your nice cool bathroom. Or would you rather have drinking chocolate?"

"No, cherries," Flora heard her mother reply, as she closed the flat door behind her and went downstairs.

After Flora had gone, they took their hot drinks down into the garden, Anita still requesting unseasonal cherries, and watched the puppy gambolling about in the flower bed, uprooting a Michaelmas daisy or two and squatting on the lawn.

"Oh, she's a good little thing, no trouble at all," Milly said, watching as the puppy dragged a hydrangea cutting up by the roots and set off with it into the orchard. "They're very intelligent, these poodle bitches."

By lunchtime the puppy was exhausted and fell asleep under the kitchen table, while Milly searched the refrigerator for something to cook. Anita went off to the lavatory.

She remembered there was something the boy had said. You took off the lid, like this, that was it. And then you poured the water from the bottle or anything else into it as you flushed. She was pleased with herself for remembering this ritual. There wasn't a bottle she could empty though. She could take water from the tap, but it was supposed to be in a jug or something. She saw a big round bowl by the bath. It was quite heavy but she managed to pick it up and heave its contents into the cistern. Then she flushed.

She enjoyed her lunch and fed bits of it to the puppy which had woken up and was taking an interest in food.

"Can she stay always?" she asked.

"Oh, no, love, she belongs to another family, bless you. But I'll bring her tomorrow."

"And the next day?"

"And the next day and the one after too, if you like. Now how about you have a nice rest while I wash up? I'll just give the goldfish his feed. He has a pinch of something or other out of a carton."

She took the little drum of fishfood out of her bag and went into the bathroom. Fish and bowl were nowhere to be seen.

"Anita," she called out, coming back into the sitting room. "What's happened to the goldfish?"

Anita shook her head.

"Don't know about fish," she said. "No fish."

"But you must have moved it. I left it there by the bath."

Then she noticed it, the empty bowl on the floor by the lavatory. She also noticed that the cistern lid was half off. She lifted it up and peered inside. No sign of the goldfish. Tentatively she lifted the lavatory lid. The goldfish was there but hardly moving; the journey from cistern to pan hadn't done it much good.

"Oh, Anita, you naughty thing," Milly reprimanded. "Well, I suppose that if it dies I'll have to try and match it up at the pet shop. I'll get a ladle from the kitchen."

When she'd gone off to hunt for a ladle, Anita bent over and scooped the goldfish up in her two hands, then she walked across to the kitchen, holding as much water as she could between closed fingers, knowing that water was what it required, being a fish.

"Here's a ladle, just the thing, oh—"

The puppy pushed between Milly's legs and bumped into Anita who dropped the fish, which slithered along the landing

197

to the top of the stairs. Anita and the puppy ran after it, the puppy tripping Anita up so that she trod on the goldfish, skidded, clutched at the banister, missed it and fell all the way down to the bottom.

Twenty-Eight

O nce settled in her office, Flora forgot all her worries about what was going on at home. The morning was spent having discussions with her fellow authors and editors, chaired by the head of the project, whom she already knew and liked. Edgar Monroe couldn't be there, but rang her afterwards.

"How did it all go?" he asked.

"Very well."

"I want to hear all about it. How about coming out for lunch? I shan't make a habit of asking you, I promise, but your first day is something to celebrate."

"I'm sorry, I've just rung for sandwiches to be sent up."

He laughed.

"The thing about sandwiches is that they can always be unordered," he told her. "I'll be with you in five minutes."

He took her to the same restaurant as before; over the broth and garlic bread, she told him about the meeting.

"I didn't realise you hadn't decided which Prime Minister you'd start with," she said.

He looked surprised.

"I assumed Pitt, of course."

"Godfrey Fielding has an idea that if this works well, he could do three great eighteenth-century Prime Ministers, Walpole, Chatham and then the younger Pitt as the third. He feels Pitt is better understood in the context of the previous century."

"Well, he would, wouldn't he? That's his period. I expect he told you that in his view Walpole was the first Prime Minister, anyway."

"He did. And I said Walpole always denied being anything of the sort and he said that proved his point and since when did Prime Ministers deny things unless they were true?"

Edgar laughed.

"I can't help but like the man," he said. "Cussed though he is. He shall do our William Pitt but it will be as the first of the nineteenth-century premiers, not the last of the eighteenth."

"Oh, I do think it's a wonderfully exciting project," she told him as the salmon was served. "I'm really so lucky to be involved. And to have Peel for my subject too."

"We're lucky to have you, my dear," he told her, raising his glass to her.

"I do hate this business of the millennium," she said suddenly.

"Why?"

She didn't really know why. She had spoken from the heart and now had to try to rationalise what she felt.

"You see," she began slowly, "the twentieth century is our century and so long as we were in it, somehow the nineteenth century didn't seem so very far away. 'It was only the end of the last century,' we could say of Gladstone's Home Rule Bills or whatever, but now it's pushed back and a mere two or three years can make it seem an extra hundred years ago. So it'll be as remote to the young as the eighteenth century was to us at their age."

"Then you must write about it in a way which makes it seem as real as their own day."

"Ah, but the young are very snobbish about the here and now, Edgar. They don't really believe that anything that happened before they were born can have been very important or that the people who lived then were quite as real as people now. Don't you remember feeling that yourself when you were young? I know I did."

"Isn't that understandable?"

"Yes, but so illogical. Why should we think that the present is so special just because we happen to have been born into it? After all, what is the present? It's only the past in the making."

He looked at her, smiled, took her hand.

"It's going to be wonderful working with you," he said. "And you look so much better than you did on your last visit," he added.

Back in her office, she thought about what he had said. It was true, she did feel much better, more alive. She seemed to be using a part of her brain which hadn't been used for ages. It was as if something of herself had lain dormant and was now being stirred into life. It was a long time since she had had the kind of conversation she'd had over lunch with Edgar; for months it had been nothing but talk of money and litigation or nonsensical chat with her mother. With renewed enthusiasm she turned back to the notes of this morning's meeting which the secretary had just brought in.

The telephone rang. When she picked it up she heard sounds of hysteria coming down the line. Milly seemed to be trying to convey a message about a fish and an ambulance, while in the background a dog barked furiously.

"I'm afraid I must go home immediately," she told the secretary, getting up and leaving the unread notes on her desk.

Twenty-Nine

T here weren't many people at the crematorium for her
mother's funeral.

The matron of the respite home was there with one of her
staff, Flora observed gratefully as she walked with her children up the aisle, and one or two family friends. Mr Hardcastle was sitting discreetly at the back, and seated together
were a few elderly strangers, presumably figures from the past,
colleagues, or even fans, of Anita Montrose, who had read of
her death in the newspaper. Milly Chatterton had come of
course and, to her surprise, Flora saw Edgar Monroe among
the congregation.

The singing was less strained and embarrassed than she'd
feared. She'd chosen familiar hymns; both Liz and Nick had
good voices and led strongly from the front pew. Somewhere
behind her she thought she could detect Edgar Monroe's rich
tenor and the duo from the respite home sang powerfully,
presumably well accustomed to such occasions.

She had given a few notes to the clergyman in charge of the
service and he spoke of Anita's career in what he called the
media, though he was surely too young ever to have heard or
seen her. But then he was so smooth-cheeked and had such a
lot of thick, bouncy dark hair that perhaps he looked younger
than he really was.

"I thought it was awfully spooky, the way the coffin glided
off," Nick said afterwards to Liz as they walked under the
cloisters to look at the bouquets of flowers.

"Yes, sinister, wasn't it? And somehow not suitable for

Gran. I mean she wasn't one for discreetly sliding away, was she? Crashing down the stairs was more her style."

"What do we do next, Liz?"

"Mum's invited everyone back home for tea, so we'd better get moving."

"OK. I'll drive."

So Liz sat in the back with her mother, while Nick drove them home.

"It was good of you both to come back," Flora said. "But you really didn't need to, you know. I didn't want you to have to uproot yourselves so near the beginning of term, when you'd just settled in."

"Oh, but we wanted to see Gran off," Liz assured her. "It'll be quite odd without her."

"It's funny how being related to someone who's died makes you seem so important," Nick said, over his shoulder. "I mean everyone stood back for us and made way. They'd never have done that if she'd still been alive."

"If she'd still been alive, we wouldn't have been there, silly."

"I know, Liz, but I'm only saying—"

"Could you just concentrate on the driving, Nick?" Flora interrupted. "I do want to be back before the others start arriving."

"If you wanted to be quick you should have let me drive," Liz told her.

"Quick and dead probably," Nick put in.

"Quite an apt pun in the circumstances," his sister told him.

"What do you mean?"

"Two meanings of quick, of course." She laughed. "You and Dad are quite hopeless; you're always making puns without realising it."

She stopped, horrified at what she'd said.

Flora took her hand.

"It's all right," she said. "I felt it too, that he wasn't with us."

Liz nodded. She realised now why she had wept in the service; it wasn't for the death of her grandmother, but the absence of her father on this family occasion. Just when she'd got over his departure too, she thought, biting her lip, angry with herself.

"Well, we're the first back," Nick said, turning the car up the drive and into the garage.

"Golly, it looks as if you've been baking for the funeral feast for weeks, Mum," Liz said, going into the kitchen and surveying the sandwiches, cakes and scones on the table. "They'll never eat all this lot."

"You'll be surprised," Flora told her, filling kettles.

She began removing covers from the food, "I thought they could collect their cups of tea in here and then go off into the drawing room," she explained, "and you and Nick can hand the food round, if you don't mind. Or they might want to go outside. It's warm enough."

In the event the guests all crowded into the drawing room. Milly was the first to arrive.

"Of course, I feel awful about it," she began, addressing the three of them in the kitchen.

"Please, Milly," Flora said, for what seemed the hundredth time. "I've told you it wasn't your fault at all. It could have happened at any time. If anything it was my fault for having wooden floors on the landing. She mightn't have slipped if it had been carpeted."

"Well, yes, I daresay. There is that. But you know how it is: if somebody's killed when they're with you, you always feel responsible," Milly said, as if precipitating a companion's death was a daily occurrence with her.

"And as for the puppy," she went on, "she was very fond of it and it didn't mean any harm, but I'm glad its owners are back home now. Thanks, Liz, they look very tempting," she said, taking two sandwiches. "Mind you," she went on, "they had worse weather in Ibiza than we've had in England. I always think it's disappointing to spend all that money on a holiday and then be no better off than if you'd stayed at home and not bothered."

Other cars were drawing up outside.

"Would you like to come into the drawing room, Milly?" Nick suggested in answer to a look from his mother.

He led her away and sat her down in an easy chair.

"I mean it's not just the money, is it," she went on, not at all deflected by the change of location. "It's all the fuss and bother of packing and travelling and all the washing when you get back too. As I said to Bobby last time, 'We don't make half as many dirty clothes when we're at home as we do on holiday. It's nothing unusual to do three cycles in the machine after just a week away.' But anyway I'm glad the Thomsons are back and have taken their puppy off me. To be honest I was glad to see the back of it, not that it meant any harm."

She drew breath to bite into a sandwich and Nick made the most of the opportunity to escape back to the kitchen.

Liz was bringing Mr Hardcastle into the drawing room. She introduced him to Milly and hung around, eager to observe the interaction of two such incompatibles.

"It's very sad, isn't it?" Milly began. "Poor Anita gone, you never know when it'll be, do you? Of course, it happens to all of us in the end, but it was a shock I can tell you. Lying there all of a heap, she was and I never did get round to replacing the goldfish."

"Do I assume, Mrs Chatterton," Mr Hardcastle asked in his precise way, "that you were with Mrs Sutton when she died?"

"Oh, yes, we were very close, her and me," Milly said, eager to claim association with Anita on her day of days. "Of course, as you probably know, she had her little problems, poor soul, but it's nice to think she's at rest up above," she added, glancing at the ceiling.

More likely causing confusion in her eternal respite home, Liz thought as, unwillingly, she left them together and went back to the kitchen. The others were converging on the drawing room now, holding cups of tea and plates.

"You go and talk to them, Mum," Liz said, "Nick can see to the handing round now and I'll fill up teacups."

Considering that there were no more than twenty people sitting and standing in the drawing room, they made a surprising amount of noise, Flora thought as she went to join them.

"I feel I should be helping," Matron said, coming up to her. "There must be something I can do."

"No, you're a guest today," Flora told her. "And thank you for coming to the service."

"I expect you're like me," Milly said, joining them. "I always enjoy a nice funeral. And it *was* very nice, though small and I thought the vicar spoke very well. Such a good-looking young man too."

Flora moved towards a little group of men and women whom she assumed to be old colleagues of her mothers.

"Did Anita ever marry again?" she heard one of them ask.

"No," the other replied. "She went freelance after her divorce."

She smiled. It reminded her of the conversations, brittle and often malicious, that she had heard as a child in her mother's house; it took her back over the years, that snatch of conversation did.

"You must be Anita's daughter, of course," one of the women said. "I remember meeting you when you were a student, you'd just come back from France and were very shy. I expect you've quite forgotten it."

Oh no, she would never forget the agony of that dinner party, the humiliation of being shown up as stupid in front of her mother's clever friends. Her mother was dead now, her friends old and unthreatening, yet still she could remember that night and feel again the awful shame of it.

"I didn't even know Anita had a daughter," she heard another woman say to one of the men in the group.

And then she saw that the man was David. She had seen him briefly at the crematorium and not recognised him, he looked so much older than she'd have expected. In fact it was the resemblance to his father – that same shock of grey hair and dark circles under the eyes – that struck her now. She turned away, amazed that he should have come.

"Come and meet Edgar Monroe," she said to Liz.

"You're Mum's new boss, aren't you?" Liz said, shaking his hand.

He smiled.

"No, her fellow-worker," he said.

"Tell me what she's working on," Liz said. "She's too modest to tell me."

Flora left them, knowing Liz would talk more easily without her mother there.

She was crossing over to talk to Matron by the window, when David came over to her.

"I thought you didn't remember me," he began.

"I didn't, at first."

"I haven't weathered as well as you have," he told her, smiling and suddenly seeming just the same as he had all those years ago, as he looked her appreciatively up and down. "You're looking wonderful. In fact you're lovelier now than when you were a girl."

"Didn't you always prefer older women?" she asked sharply, because after all why should she be considerate and tactful? If you can't speak the truth on the day of your mother's funeral, when can you?

He did have the grace, she observed with satisfaction, to look abashed.

"I'm sorry," he said. "If I hurt you. But it was a long time ago."

"Oh, don't be sorry. I was well out of it. You'd probably have treated me like you treated my mother."

"I'm so glad to know you've had a good marriage," he went on, determinedly polite. "I've talked to both your children and they're delightful, they really are a credit to you."

"And yours? Do you have children?"

207

"I had a boy by my first marriage, whom I don't see as he stayed with his mother. And a girl by my second marriage. I do see her now and then but she spends most of the time with her mother who has remarried and lives in America."

"I'm sorry," she said and, to her surprise, meant it.

"It's a lovely house you have here," he said, "and the garden is beautiful."

They both stood for a moment looking down the autumn garden. The lawn was looking good, thanks to Mr Woodcock's recent visit, the hydrangeas were heavy with flowers, the herbaceous bed still bright with Michaelmas daisies, phlox and chrysanthemums. Late roses still lingered in the rose bed.

"It's getting warm in here," she said. "Let's open the french doors."

He opened them for her and they stepped outside on to the terrace.

"There's a lot of work in all this," he said, looking about him. "Is your husband a keen gardener? Or, have I got it wrong? You're a widow?"

"No, divorced," she said, slightly predating the case.

"I'm sorry." He paused, puzzled. "I thought you'd had a happy marriage?"

"I did," she told him and walked away to join the others.

Matron, neat in navy blue and white, was putting on her gloves.

"We must be on our way," she said. "Thank you for letting us join your family this afternoon. We shall miss Anita's visits to us. She always looked so colourful. And she was often quite lively to talk to." ·

The others spoke similarly as one by one they took their leave.

"I shall see you next Monday," she told Edgar.

"Now don't push yourself if you're busy here," he said, his craggy face looking down at her with kindly concern. "I know there's always a lot to do."

"I shall see to things over the weekend."

"Until Monday then," he said, and kissed her.

Martin Hardcastle had retrieved his umbrella from the stand in the hall and now returned to say his farewells.

"Thank you for your hospitality," he said, holding out his hand. "I shall be writing to you about the matters we discussed earlier this week. Then, if I may, I shall visit you again for the signing of forms."

"I shall be at home on Tuesdays and Thursdays."

"Then perhaps you will let me have the pleasure of taking you out to lunch after we have finished with business matters?"

"Which you always find tedious and boring despite the skill with which you manage them?" she said, laughing up at him.

He smiled, that cautious half smile that she had come to expect from such remarks, a surprisingly puckish little smile that consisted more of a brightening of the eye and a slight twisting of the mouth than in any larger contortion of the features in the smooth-skinned face.

"Nothing concerning Mrs Sutton's affairs could ever be that," he told her.

Milly was almost the last to leave.

"As I say, I'm really sorry—" she began.

"We want to thank you, Milly, for all you did," Flora interrupted, before she could start yet again on her usual theme.

"Well, I only did what anyone would have done. I mean calling the doctor and the ambulance. And the police and the fire brigade," she added.

"The fire brigade? I didn't know—"

"Well, it was just an impulse really, when I saw her down there. I thought now how do we move her and I remembered hearing about a fireman's lift, so I rang them, but when I told them the details, they said they thought I'd be all right with just the doctor and the ambulance men."

"And the police?"

"They said the same really, but they seemed glad to have

been informed. You can get a lot really, from one 999 call. And they're free."

"I wonder if you'd like to take some of these cakes home with you, Milly?" Flora said, beginning to put some into a bag.

"Oh, I wouldn't say no. Just the thing for Bobby's tea. I see," she said, dropping her voice as Flora escorted her out to the car, "that Duncan didn't come to the funeral."

"Perhaps he didn't know."

"Oh, Bobby told him, I made a point of that, in case he didn't see it in the papers. I mean she was his mother-in-law, after all. Blood," she added illogically as she got into the car, "is thicker than water, I always say. But there, I expect he had other things on his mind."

Flora stood for a moment waving her off and hoping that the relief she felt didn't show too clearly on her face, then she went back into the kitchen.

"I hope you don't mind, I asked your daughter to take me on a tour of the garden," David said, coming in with Liz.

"I told him you wouldn't mind, Mum, so long as he admired it and said how hard you must work. I'll go and start on the drawing room."

Flora laughed, but after Liz had left she turned to him and said, "Why did you come?"

"Because I once promised your mother that I would come to her funeral," he said.

So it was as simple as that.

"Tell Mum what Milly said to you about the goldfish," Liz instructed her brother, who was sitting next to her on the old couch in the kitchen, while Flora put away the remains of the tea.

He laughed.

"No, you tell, you're better at imitating her."

Flora looked from one to the other.

"Well, one of you get on with it," she said.

"She said to Nick, and I heard her, 'I told a white lie, Nick. Yes, I told the Thomsons it had died of natural causes. Well, I didn't want to incriminate your poor dear grandmother who wasn't what you'd call responsible for her actions, was she?'"

Liz was a good mimic; she exactly caught Milly Chatterton's breathless self-righteousness.

"'They were very nice about it,'" Liz's imitation continued, "'and said it was quite elderly. Well, elderly for a goldfish, I mean. I hope I did right to say it had died a natural death. Really, what else could I say, Nick?'"

They were leaning against each other, these children of hers, laughing helplessly. Just like when they were little in the bouncer.

"She could have said it had committed suicide," Nick managed to suggest, before being convulsed again.

"Being Milly she could have said it had done it by drowning itself," Liz shrieked.

Flora shook her head at them, but couldn't resist joining in.

"She could have said she tried to give it the kiss of life and accidentally swallowed it," she said collapsing with them on the couch.

It was very quiet after they left the next morning. But, Flora said to herself, as, having dropped her children off at the station, she returned to the empty house, I am managing better than I did after their first departure. In time I shall get accustomed to being on my own; already I am looking back less than I did. She smiled as she realised how often nowadays she addressed herself in the manner of one encouraging a friend. *You are doing very well, my dear*, she seemed to be saying.

And how well Liz and Nick had done too. She'd been wrong to think that their upbringing hadn't prepared them for the shock and disillusionment of their father's abrupt disappearance, without explanation or leave-taking; it had in fact given them the strength to weather it. Nothing could take away the joyful confidence that a secure and happy childhood had given them, just as nothing could bestow it upon herself who had been deprived of one.

There was coffee left in the pot; she warmed it and took it outside; five minutes to compose myself before I start sorting out the flat, she thought, before I start clearing away the remains of my mother.

She had been so busy organising the funeral, she told herself, that she'd scarcely paused to think about the woman who had died, the pathetic old woman who had once had such power over her. No, she realised that she wasn't being honest. It wasn't that she hadn't had time; the truth was that she had shied away from thinking about her, not wanting to admit to herself that she had felt no real grief at the death of this woman who had been neither wife to her husband nor mother to her only child.

And yet she was sad; sad for what might have been. If only for a little while Anita Montrose had made her husband happy, how different it might all have been. As it was, she could never remember a time when her father was not a sad man, beyond his daughter's power to help or make happy. Her own childhood had been wretched too, but it was for her father that she had always grieved, not herself. When Philip Larkin wrote, "They fuck you up, your mum and dad," he only said the half of it; they fuck each other up too.

Now that she no longer had to look after a mother whom she cared for out of duty, not love, she really could at last draw a line under the past, make a clean break with her parents, just as the lawyers had arranged for her to make a clean break with her husband. Think positive, Flora, count the blessings of freedom for you are an orphan now and soon to be a divorcee.

For she had to admit to herself as she walked around the garden, coffee mug in hand, that now that the money was sorted out, the benefits of being Duncanless were beginning to make themselves evident. She shouldn't have been shocked by the dismay she'd felt when, on that brief encounter with Duncan on the landing at Tilley's, she'd realised she didn't want him back. Of course she didn't want to give up her new-found freedom, even if it had been forced upon her. She enjoyed having her bedroom to herself and she'd got used to not having to shape her day to his needs. Henceforward she could arrange work or leisure to suit herself. She could spend – or not spend – on house or garden or anything else as required. She'd found that she liked making her own decisions without having to consult him. In fact it wasn't just her bedroom that she enjoyed having to herself; it was having her whole life to herself. "You must learn to be selfish," a friend had advised. And, oh yes, she was learning.

She never would have thought she would come to feel this, she who had given her life to making a good home for her husband and children, she who had cooked and baked, washed, ironed and mended with such zeal for all these years. But she did. She was harder, tougher now, she knew that. Nothing would make her give up her independence now that she had fought the good fight and won it. What possessed people to remarry? It was, of course, nice to be taken out by the likes of Martin Hardcastle and Edgar Monroe but she would never want to be married again. She'd done that bit; time to move on. Or maybe it was just a case of once bitten twice shy.

No, not even a paragon with the wit of Martin, the kindliness and scholarship of Edgar and the dangerous sexiness of David all rolled into one gorgeous male would make her ever again depend on another man for her happiness and security. An affair was one thing; matrimony another. The former would suit her now, never again the latter. This is one of those things, she thought, for which the old have cause to bless the young for showing us the way.

It was very still as she walked around the sunlit garden, thinking these things, while no wind stirred the fresh autumn air. This Friday morning, she suddenly realised, might be just

213

the day for going to White Horse Hill to carry out, at last, her
father's wishes.

She had done the journey before so the route was familiar as
she made her way along the M25 and the M4, the ashes sitting
on the passenger seat beside her, securely fastened with the
safety belt around them.

After she left the motorway, the road was narrow and
wound its way between villages with thatched cottages and
signs which warned of ducks crossing the road and whose
names read like a poem: Wanborough and Liddington, Hinton
Parva and Bishopstone, Idstone and Ashbury.

At Ashbury she stopped for lunch at the Rose and Crown,
seating herself on a bench by the window, looking out at a neat
row of thatched cottages. She had left the ashes strapped into
the passenger seat; in a novel, she thought, the car would be
stolen and the ashes with it, and my mission would be aborted,
but this is real life and I shall finish my onion soup and my
glass of red wine, which as a motorist I should not be having,
and be on my way to White Horse Hill.

She drove slowly, beginning to feel a sense of occasion,
which increased after she turned up the lane which led up to
the hill. After all, scattering parental ashes is not something
one can do often in one's life.

The car park was deserted as she undid the safety belt and
lifted the ashes into a big wicker basket she'd brought with her
for the purpose. Nor was there a soul to be seen as she made
her way through the little gate and up into the fields beyond.
Only a few sheep which wandered about on the hillside looked
up to stare as she passed.

The way was steep and the basket surprisingly heavy; surely
it must be urns and not ashes which weigh so much, she
thought, pausing now and then as she climbed, partly to rest
and partly to gaze in awe at the scenery all around her. It was a
panorama of five counties which unfolded below her like a
map, the distant fields looking small and neatly parcelled, the

nearby valley furrowed and terraced. It seemed timeless, this great sweep of English countryside, in which in every direction she could see an undulating landscape of little hills and dales dotted with ancient settlements, clumps of trees and isolated farms.

In all this grandeur she felt herself to be a very small thing, a little piece of humanity moving ant-like about its business. And so, frequently changing the basket from hand to hand, she reached the horse itself, which looked nothing like a horse at close quarters. Only from a distance had its iron age creators made it seem to stride across the hillside.

The sheep-cropped grass was springy and good to walk on. She climbed a little further towards the ancient earthworks which for centuries had stood watch over the hill and found a hollow where she could sit. There she settled down and took the top off the urn which held her father's ashes. Then she took the other urn and carefully tipped the remains of her mother into his urn. Then she replaced the cover and shook them both violently together.

A light breeze was blowing now; it was very gentle but, remembering her father's warning, she took care not to stand downwind as she released to the elements all that remained of her parents. Whatever they were in life, she thought as she scattered their mingled ashes on to the bright green turf, in death they have become inseparable. She smiled at the thought, knowing that it would have delighted her father and infuriated her mother.

Then she replaced the urns in the basket and, without a backward glance, made her way down the hill to the car park.